D0407378

Veterans
Way

Veterans Way

HART'S CROSSING SERIES #2

Robin Lee Hatcher

Revell
Grand Rapids, Michigan

© 2005 by Robin Lee Hatcher

Published by Fleming H. Revell
a division of Baker Publishing Group
P.O. Box 6287, Grand Rapids, MI 49516-6287

Printed in the United States of America

All rights reserved. No part of this publication may be reproduced, stored in a re-
trieval system, or transmitted in any form or by any means—for example, electronic,
photocopy, recording—without the prior written permission of the publisher. The
only exception is brief quotations in printed reviews.

Library of Congress Cataloging-in-Publication Data
Hatcher, Robin Lee.
    Veterans way / Robin Lee Hatcher.
        p.   cm. — (Hart's Crossing ; Bk. 2)
    ISBN 0-8007-1855-0
    1. World War, 1939–1945—Veterans—Fiction. 2. Older people—
Fiction. 3. First loves—Fiction. I. Title. II. Series: Hatcher, Robin Lee.
Hart's Crossing ; v. #2.
PS3558.A73574V47 2005
813'.54—dc22   2004026773

Scripture is taken from the *Holy Bible*, New Living Translation, copyright © 1996.
Used by permission of Tyndale House Publishers, Inc., Wheaton, Illinois 60189.
All rights reserved.

To those who dare to love—
at any age, in any season.

Love never gives up, never loses faith, is always
  hopeful,
and endures through every circumstance.

1 Corinthians 13:7

PROLOGUE

August 14, 1945

Stephanie would never forget the jubilation that raced through Hart's Crossing, Idaho, at the end of World War II. People danced in the streets and blew horns and whooped and hollered and set off fireworks. As a nine-year-old, she couldn't quite grasp the significance of everything her parents and other adults said about V-J Day, but she understood something wonderful had happened.

So did ten-year-old Jimmy.

Maybe that's why he gave Stephanie her first boy-girl kiss right there outside the Apollo Movie Theater on that warm August night. The kiss might not have been as dramatic as the photograph she would see later on the cover of *Life* magazine, the one of that sailor bending a nurse over his arm and kissing her on the lips. But that didn't stop Stephanie's heart from racing, and it didn't stop her from deciding, right then and there, that she was going to marry Jimmy Scott when she grew up.

CHAPTER ONE

Stephanie Watson loved autumn, especially the warm and hazy butter-yellow days of Indian summer.

For what seemed the first time since her husband Chuck's death last year, she took pleasure in the beauty of her surroundings as she walked along the street toward town. The leaves on the trees that lined the thoroughfare were turning yellow, gold, orange, and red, and flowerbeds wore a spectacular coat of riotous colors.

Why, she wondered, did nature's palette seem more vibrant in autumn?

Next year, she would plant chrysanthemums along the front of her house. And asters. She was partial to asters. She hadn't gardened this year. Last spring, the idea of watering and weeding all summer long seemed far more than she could manage. But next year? Yes, next year she would be ready.

Her widowed friends had told her things would get better, that even though she continued to miss her husband of fifty years, time would dull the pain. She hadn't believed them at first. She hadn't believed them for a long while. But it seemed they were right. The pain in her heart was less, and the memories in her mind were sweeter.

Stephanie was thankful to God for that.

Bells chimed overhead as she opened the door to Terri's Tangles Beauty Salon. Terri Sampson glanced over her shoulder, her hands busy with blow-dryer and brush as she finished styling Till Hart's silver-gray hair.

"Please tell me you're early, Steph." Terri's gaze darted to the clock on the wall.

"I am. It's such a beautiful day, I hated to stay indoors another minute. So I decided to walk over."

Stephanie met Till's gaze in the mirror. "Good morning, Till. How are you?"

"I'm dandy, thanks. And you?"

"I'm good, too."

Till and Stephanie had known each other since they were girls. Both of them had lived their entire lives in this sleepy little town on the plains of southern Idaho. The two women had many things in common, many of the same beliefs, likes and dislikes. But while Till, the granddaughter of the town's founder, had never married, Stephanie had been married nearly all of her life.

Memories of Chuck flashed in her mind, and she felt a bittersweet warmth in her chest. How she missed him. Missed his wry sense of humor. Missed the gentle touch of his hand beneath her elbow as they crossed the street. Missed his grumpy complaints as he searched for his ever-misplaced eyeglasses.

Terri turned off the blow-dryer, bringing a sudden silence to the beauty shop.

After a moment, Till said, "Steph, you'll never guess who's returned to Hart's Crossing to live." She didn't wait for an answer. "James Scott. Can you imagine?

11

After all of these years, he's decided to move back to Idaho." Till looked at Terri. "You know the big blue house on Horizon Street?"

"The Patterson house?"

"That's the one. Only the Pattersons didn't own it. It's belonged to the Scott family since it was built back in the late thirties. The Pattersons rented it for twenty years."

Stephanie sat on one of the chairs attached to a hair dryer. "I didn't know the Scotts still owned that house. I thought it was sold after Mrs. Scott went to live in Seattle with James and his wife."

"No." Till shook her head. "Betty Frazier has been managing it for them for at least a decade. She was chomping at the bit to sell it, too. It would have brought her realty firm a very nice commission. I can tell you, she *never* expected James to return to live in it. Who would? Not after fifty years."

"Fifty-two years," Stephanie corrected. "He was eighteen when he went into the army."

Till leaned toward Terri and, in a stage whisper, said, "Steph and James were sweet on each other when they were kids. Everyone except his mother called him

Jimmy back then. My, oh my. What a handsome fellow he was."

Terri's eyes widened with interest. "Is that right, Steph? You had a boyfriend before Mr. Watson? I can't picture that."

"After fifty years with Chuck, it's hard for me to imagine it either." Stephanie smiled. "But it's true. Jimmy Scott was my first love."

Terri sat on the second dryer chair. "Tell me more. You know there's no keeping secrets in a hair salon."

Stephanie allowed memories to drift through her mind—sweet, innocent, misty. Goodness, who was that girl she'd been and when had she become the white-haired woman she saw in the mirror today? It seemed only yesterday that Jimmy Scott kissed her outside the Apollo Movie Theater. But yesterday was actually sixty years ago.

"Well?" Terri prompted.

"I was his best friend when we were in elementary school, and when I was nine, I decided I was going to marry him. That was the night he gave me my first kiss." She laughed softly. "We dated all through high school, and by then everyone else expected us to get married, too."

"So what happened? Why didn't you marry him?"

"For one thing, he never asked me. He meant to, I think, but he never did. After he went into the army, we corresponded, but then I met Chuck and he stole my heart."

"And you had to write Mr. Scott a Dear John letter?" Terri looked from Stephanie to Till and back again. "How awful for him."

Stephanie shook her head. "Actually, he'd met someone, too. It all turned out for the best. If he hadn't gone away, I might not have married Chuck, and James might not have married Martha. They were together almost as many years as Chuck and I."

"James lost his wife about three years ago," Till told Terri as she rose from the styling chair, patting her hair with her right hand. "To cancer. I heard she was ill for a long time before passing. Must have been terribly hard on him and their children, losing her that way."

As difficult as losing Chuck was for Stephanie, she was thankful her husband hadn't suffered. He'd enjoyed good health right up to the end. On the day he died, he'd played a round of golf, come home, sat in his easy chair, and slipped into the presence of Jesus.

Till stepped toward the cash register. "What's the damage, Terri?"

"Fifteen today, Miss Hart."

"You need to raise your prices, young lady." Till placed two bills on the counter, a twenty and a five. "A worker is worthy of her wage, you know." She gave a farewell wave to Stephanie, then left the salon.

"Just give me a minute to sweep up, Steph, and then we'll get you started."

"No hurry. Take your time."

Time was one thing Stephanie had plenty of these days.

James Scott stood in the living room of his boyhood home, wondering if he was as crazy as his children thought. Why would a man in his right mind leave the city where he'd lived and worked for more than forty-five years to return to a small town like Hart's

Crossing? That's what his son and eldest daughter had asked several times over the past few weeks. James had a hard time giving Kurt or Jenna an answer, mainly because he wasn't sure himself.

James and his wife, Martha, had loved living in Washington State. They'd owned a lovely home in Bremerton, purchased long before Seattle area housing prices shot through the roof. All three of their children—Kurt, Jenna, and Paula—had been raised in that four-bedroom home, and it was there Martha had breathed her last one windy March morning more than three years before.

Maybe if his kids and grandkids lived in the Pacific Northwest, James would have remained in Bremerton. But Kurt and his family had settled in Pennsylvania after a series of job-related moves; Jenna lived in England with her husband of five years; and Paula, a divorced mom of two, had a home in Florida. Visits to Washington were few and far between for all of them. James understood. They had busy lives of their own.

"But Hart's Crossing, Dad?" Jenna had made it sound like the end of the world. "You haven't been back there since Grandma Scott moved in with you

16

and Mom. I was still a teenager, for Pete's sake. Why not move into a nice retirement community? There's got to be some good ones in your area. That way you can still be near your friends."

"I have a few friends in Idaho, too," he'd answered her. "Besides, the cost of living is less there, and I own that house free and clear."

"Dad, you're not having money problems, are you?"

That comment had irritated him. Did she think he was in his dotage? "No, Jenna. I'm not. But thanks for asking."

His daughter might live halfway around the globe, but James had been able to imagine the exasperated expression on her face at the end of that phone call.

Well, it was done now. His kids would have to accept his decision, like it or not.

The doorbell rang. James was glad for the interruption. He needed to stop woolgathering and resume his unpacking. He pulled open the door and discovered a woman on the stoop. "Yes?"

"Jimmy Scott, it really is you. I heard you were back, but I needed to come see for myself."

No one had called him Jimmy in decades.

"Have I changed so much?" she asked, a twinkle appearing in her faded blue eyes.

James pushed open the screen door, peering more closely at the woman. About his age, she had a cap of curly white hair and a pleasantly round face with plenty of lines etched around her eyes and mouth. She looked familiar but he couldn't quite . . .

Then she smiled.

"Steph!"

"In the flesh."

He motioned her inside. "How are you?"

"I'm well, James. And you?"

"Good. I'm good." He went to the sofa and cleared away some of the clutter to make room for her. "Have a seat. I'd offer you a cup of coffee, but the coffeemaker isn't unpacked yet. How 'bout a glass of water?"

"I don't need a thing, thanks. I'm fine." She settled onto the couch. "I can't stay but a moment anyway."

James moved a box off his recliner and sat, too.

"I should apologize for barging in this way. But when Till told me this morning that you'd moved back to Hart's Crossing after all these years, I just

18

had to stop by to say hello. It's such a surprise. Such a nice surprise."

"My kids think I've lost my mind. Moving back to a rural town in Idaho when I could live anywhere else in the country."

She laughed. "Most adult children *would* think that insane. Tell me about them. Your children and grand-children."

James was happy to oblige. "My oldest, Kurt, lives in Pennsylvania. He and his wife have three kids, a boy and two girls. Kurt's in the computer business, but don't ask me what he does. I know just enough to send and receive email and surf the Internet a bit."

He didn't add that his son was always sending him new software to try out and that his failure to use them was a great disappointment for Kurt.

"My middle daughter, Jenna, and her husband live overseas. In England. He works for the U.S. govern-ment over there. They've been married about five years. No children yet, but they're still hoping it will happen."

Hope was a mild word for what his daughter felt. Jenna ached for a baby. But at forty-one, she heard her biological clock like the *bong* of Big Ben, and her childlessness had left her angry at God.

"My youngest, Paula, got divorced last year. She's a school teacher living in Florida with her two daughters."

James wasn't sorry his philandering ex-son-in-law was out of the picture, but his heart broke whenever he spoke to Paula and heard the lingering sadness in her voice. He wished he could make it better.

Stephanie put her hands together in front of her chin, almost a clap but not quite. "Five grandchildren. How wonderful for you."

"What about your family?" he replied.

"My daughter, Miranda, has made me a grandmother of two, Isabella and Foster. They live right here in Hart's Crossing, so I'm quite spoiled." Her smile was gentle as she added, "It must be hard for you, having your family living so far away. Is that one of the reasons you came back to Hart's Crossing?"

"Mostly. Or maybe I'm trying to recapture a bit of my youth." He shrugged. "But I think there were just too many memories in Bremerton to stay."

Stephanie's smile faded. "I know what you mean."

James saw the sorrow that mirrored his own. "Of course you do. I heard about Chuck's passing. I'm sorry for your loss. The few times I met him, he seemed like a real nice guy."

"He was. Salt of the earth." She rose from the sofa, the sparkle gone from her eyes. "I've taken up enough of your time. I should be getting on home."

"I'm glad you stopped by." He followed her to the door. "I'm sure we'll see each other again."

She smiled. A bit halfhearted but still a smile. "In a town this size, I can guarantee it."

James watched her descend the porch steps, then closed the door and returned to work. At the rate he was going, he wouldn't find that coffeepot for another week.

"You set eternity in our hearts, Lord," Stephanie said softly as she walked toward home. "So no matter how long people live, no matter how old they are, it always feels wrong when death comes to someone we love."

She thought of James, leaving his home in Washington after all these years because there were too many memories of his departed wife. Would she do the same if her daughter and family weren't here in Hart's Crossing? Would she run away if she could?

And yet, James hadn't looked like a man who was running away. Yes, there had been a note of sadness in his voice when he'd mentioned the memories, but there had also been a strength of purpose in his gaze. He hadn't doubted his decision to return to Hart's Crossing. Not a bit.

But wasn't that always true of James? Even as a teenager, he'd seemed to know with unshakable assurance where he was to go and what he was to do. It was that certainty that had taken him away from Hart's Crossing, changing the course of both their lives.

Stephanie wondered what would be changed, now that he'd returned.

CHAPTER TWO

September was one of Stephanie Watson's two months to hostess the weekly meeting of the Thimbleberry Quilting Club. She loved having these women in her home. It made the old place feel lived in and less lonely. Most of the time, she rattled around in it like a bean in a baby's rattle.

Chuck and Stephanie's only child, Miranda, lived with her husband and two teenagers on the opposite side of Hart's Crossing—no more than two miles away—in one of the new subdivisions that had sprung up in the last few years. Miranda tried to stop by to see her mother on a regular basis, but with a job in the mayor's office and a busy family to care for, it wasn't easy.

Till Hart removed her wire-rimmed glasses and set them on the arm of her chair. "Oh, dear. My eyes do get tired these days." She shook her head. "Getting old is such a bother."

"Isn't that the truth," Francine Hunter said with an emphatic nod.

Stephanie couldn't agree more. Every year went by faster than the one before. It was enough to make an old woman dizzy. Still, if it weren't for her tired joints and miscellaneous aches and pains, she wouldn't believe she was sixty-nine. In her mind, she was no more than twenty-five or twenty-six, the same age as the club's youngest member, Patti Bedford.

"What do you think, Frani?" Ethel Jacobsen asked. "Should we start working on a wedding quilt for Angie? Hasn't Bill Palmer popped the question yet?"

Five pairs of eyes turned toward Francine, but she shook her head, disappointing them all.

"That man's besotted with your daughter," Mary Benrey, the secretary at Hart's Crossing Community

Church, said to Francine. "Why on earth is he dragging his feet?"

"Well, at first he was waiting for her to become a Christian. Now that that's happened, I think he's waiting because he's afraid she'll bolt back to California if he moves too fast. She's always been so independent. Bill's taking no chances on spooking her. They've only been dating a few months, you know."

Stephanie's thoughts drifted to the autumn she first met Chuck Watson. Jimmy Scott had been gone for four months, an eternity when a girl is seventeen and all her friends have dates on Friday nights.

She and her best friend, Wilma Milburn, were sitting in the booth closest to the door at the Over the Rainbow Diner when Owen Watson came in, accompanied by a tall, good-looking boy Stephanie hadn't seen before. Owen stopped when he saw them.

"Hi, Steph. Wilma. Meet my cousin, Chuck. He's gonna be staying with us for the next year. Chuck, this is Steph and Wilma."

Chuck Watson—broad-shouldered, golden-haired, blue-eyed—smiled at Stephanie. "A pleasure to meet you."

Unlike Bill with Angie, Chuck hadn't wasted any time. He'd asked Stephanie out that same night. When she said no because of Jimmy, he didn't give up. He pursued her relentlessly. Little gifts. Flowers. Phone calls. He wore her down with his persistence. And one day, she just couldn't say no again. After their first date, falling in love with Chuck was inevitable. They were engaged by the New Year, and their wedding was the day after her high school graduation.

Chuck's one year in Hart's Crossing with his aunt, uncle, and cousins turned into a lifetime with Stephanie. Fifty years. How blessed she'd been to be his wife.

"Did you know Mr. Scott, Frani, before he moved away?" Patti Bedford asked, catching Stephanie's attention and drawing her thoughts back to the present.

"Not really. I was only eleven when he left Hart's Crossing to go off to war. Nothing mattered to me back then but playing with my favorite dolls and trying to escape practicing the piano when my mother told me to."

All the women laughed.

"He must have been a real heartthrob when he was younger." Patti took several careful stitches before adding, "He reminds me of Sean Connery. Don't you think so? Very distinguished with that white hair and close-trimmed beard."

Stephanie frowned. She didn't think James resembled the movie star at all. He looked like . . . James. Sure, his hair was silver and thinning instead of black and thick, but he was still just an older version of the boy she'd known so long ago. Handsome, yes. But Sean Connery? She didn't see it.

"Well . . ." Till set her reading glasses onto the bridge of her nose, "one thing's for sure. His return has given folks something new to talk about."

James slid into a booth at the Over the Rainbow Diner and took a menu—one sheet of gold-colored paper encased in a plastic sleeve—from the rack beneath the window. After several days of his own rather pathetic cooking, he was ready for a meal prepared by someone else.

"Hello."

He looked up at the waitress as she set a tall glass of water on the table. An attractive woman in her early forties, she wore a white apron over a red and white striped dress that was straight out of the diner's heyday. The uniform went well with the retro decor.

"You must be Mr. Scott."

James raised an eyebrow.

She laughed. "There aren't that many strangers in town who fit your description." She held out a hand in welcome. "I'm Nancy Raney. My husband, Harry, and I own the diner."

"It looks great in here." He shook her hand. "Reminds me of when I was a boy."

"Thanks. It was pretty run down when we bought the place fifteen years ago. It took a lot of remodeling before we could reopen." She motioned with her arm, as if inviting him to inspect the interior a second time. "We tried hard to recapture the way it looked in some of the photos that folks like Miss Hart had in their albums. Photos and the memory of some who lived here in the 1940s and '50s."

"Old-timers, you mean?" He chuckled.

She pretended to be horrified. "I'd never call Miss Hart an old-timer." The twinkle in her eye gave her jest away.

"Smart girl." He glanced again at the menu. "I'll take the Scarecrow burger with a chocolate shake. Well done on the burger."

"Coming right up, Mr. Scott."

After Nancy walked away, James dropped the menu in the rack then turned his gaze out the window. Across the street was the Apollo Movie Theater. He'd noticed on the day he arrived that, like this restaurant, it appeared to have been restored, at least on the exterior. The marquee announced that one of the summer's top action films would be playing over the weekend. Maybe he'd go see it tomorrow.

The door to the diner opened, and the sound of women's voices drew his gaze away from the window.

"Well, look who's here," Till Hart said as she and Stephanie neared his booth. "James, were your ears burning? We talked about you at our quilting club meeting this morning."

Out of habit, he started to rise.

Till waved him down. "Land sakes. Don't get up for us."

"Would you care to join me for lunch?"

Till glanced at her companion, then said, "We'd love to," and slid onto the seat across from him. Stephanie sat beside her.

"Are you feeling more settled?" Till asked.

James took two menus from the rack and handed them to the women. "Yes. Although, to be honest, it's a bit strange. The house is familiar from my boyhood, and my furniture is familiar from my house in Bremerton. But the two together?" He shrugged. "They seem an odd combination."

"I can imagine they would," Stephanie replied, giving him a warm smile.

It occurred to James that she was as pretty today as she was when he kissed her on V-J Day. Granted, it was a different kind of pretty. Her face was softly wrinkled, and the freckles that had sprinkled her nose as a girl were gone. Her hair was white instead of the golden blond shade of her youth, and she wore it short and curly rather than long and straight, the way he remembered it. But the style flattered her. The one

30

thing that hadn't changed was that smile. He'd always been partial to Stephanie's smile.

Nancy arrived at the table with two more water glasses. "Hello, ladies. Joining Mr. Scott for lunch today?"

"That we are." Till pointed at the menu without having looked at it. "I'd like the Emerald City salad, please, with the dressing on the side."

"Anything to drink?"

"Water's fine, thank you."

"And you, Mrs. Watson?"

"I'll have the same, Nancy. Thanks."

More people entered the diner. A farmer in overalls and work boots. A businessman in slacks and short-sleeved shirt, sans coat and tie. Two young mothers with several toddlers in tow.

"So tell me, James," Till said. "I'm sure you're sick of the question, but I want to know. What brought you back to Hart's Crossing?"

She was right. He was sick of that question. Sick of trying to come up with an answer that sounded logical—or at least humorous. This time he didn't choose his words carefully. He just spoke from his heart.

"Till, I've been asking God what I'm supposed to do with the rest of my life ever since I retired two years ago. When the Pattersons moved out of Mother's house, it seemed like the answer to my prayers." His gaze shifted to Stephanie. "I felt like the Lord said go, so here I am."

Stephanie smiled at him once again. "It's always best when we're obedient to God's calling. Whether or not we understand it fully."

"Indeed," he said, returning her smile.

Stephanie was acquainted with many people in Hart's Crossing who shared her Christian faith. All of her closest friends trusted in Jesus for their salvation. But it seemed a special lagniappe to discover James was a believer, too.

Nancy Raney approached their booth, carrying a large brown tray above her shoulder with one hand. In the blink of an eye, she placed the two salads, hamburger platter, and milkshake on the table. "Enjoy your lunch. Let me know if you need anything else." Then she was off to wait on other customers.

Stephanie picked up her fork. "The Scarecrow is my favorite burger," she told James. "I love fried onions."

"Me, too. I'll try not to breathe on you when I'm finished." He punctuated the comment with a wink and a grin.

For goodness' sake. Stephanie caught her breath. *Patti's right.*

James did bear more than a passing resemblance to Sean Connery.

CHAPTER THREE

From: "Kurt Scott" <kurtscott@fiberpipe
              .net>
Sent: Saturday, September 24 8:16 AM
To: "James Scott" <jtscott@fiberpipe.net>
Subject: Online yet?

Hi, Dad. Just wondering if your computer is up
and running. Haven't heard from you since you
called to say you and the movers got to Hart's
Crossing okay. Directory assistance didn't
have a local number for you as of yesterday,
so I tried your cell phone but couldn't get
through. I didn't bother to leave a message. I
figured you're busy.

I wish I could take some time off to help you
move in, but it just wasn't possible right
now. Glad you understand. Don't overdo it and

hurt yourself with all that unpacking. Ask for
help or hire somebody if you need to.

The kids returned to school a month ago, and
now everybody's going a different direction
several nights a week. I remember how we
always had family dinners together when I
was a boy, and I'm wondering how you and Mom
managed that. It seems like half the time at
my house, nobody's home at the dinner hour,
let alone sitting down to eat together.

Give us a call or respond to this email when
you can. Sure hope you're not regretting your
decision to move.

Kurt

From: "James Scott" <jtscott@fiberpipe.net>
Sent: Saturday, September 24 10:32 AM
To: "Kurt & Neta" <kurtscott@fiberpipe
              .net>
Subject: Re: Online yet?

Good morning, Kurt. My telephone service
was finally up and working as of 4:45 p.m.
yesterday. My number is 208-555-4632. I set
up my trusty computer in my boyhood bedroom,
which is now serving as my office. This is the
first time I've turned it on, so I'm glad to

see it's working. The worst of the unpacking
is done, and except for a few minor aches
and pains (which could be my age more than
anything else), I'm feeling fine. You don't
have to worry about me. I still have a modicum
of good sense in this head of mine.

I had lunch today with two old friends. I
haven't seen either of them in more than
twenty years. Even when your grandmother was
still living in Hart's Crossing, our paths
didn't cross much. As you might guess, we
had a lot of catching up to do. We did a
fair share of reminiscing about the "good old
days."

I'd planned to go to a movie later today, but
I was invited to see the local high school
football team—the Hart's Crossing Hornets—
play against one of its biggest rivals, the
Sawtooth Pioneers. (They were rivals fifty
years ago, too. Some things never change.)
Since the weather is good, I thought I'd do
that. Go, Hornets!

I'll call you soon.

Love, Dad

Stephanie was not a huge fan of football, but she *was* a huge fan of her grandson, Foster. This was his first at home game as part of the senior varsity football team. There was no way she would miss seeing him play today, short of a blizzard in September. Judging by the clear blue sky overhead and the warm breeze rustling the trees in her front yard, she needn't fear snow.

When the doorbell rang a few minutes before noon, Stephanie grabbed her jacket, lap blanket, and purse on her way to answer it.

The door opened before she got there. "It's me, Grandma," Isabella called. "Are you ready?"

"I'm ready, dear." She received her seventeen-year-old granddaughter's quick hug and peck on the cheek. "Are your parents with you?"

"No. Mom had some work to do at the office. She said she'll meet us at the school before the game starts, but I wouldn't bet on it. You know how she forgets everything else when she's working." She gave a little shrug, as if denying the disappointment in her voice. "Dad's helping with the concessions, so he went early with Foster."

Stephanie and Isabella stepped onto the porch, and Stephanie pulled the front door closed behind her, pausing to be sure it was locked.

"I like your jogging suit, Grandma. That blue matches your eyes. Where'd you get it?"

"From the Coldwater Creek catalog."

They walked to the curb, where Isabella had parked her Subaru Outback.

"Dear," Stephanie said as she opened the passenger side door, "I hope you don't mind, but I offered to pick up an old friend of mine. He's just returned to Hart's Crossing, and I invited him to come see Foster play."

"No trouble." Isabella slipped into the driver's seat. "Where does he live?"

"On Horizon Street."

"I can get there off of Pine, right?"

"Yes." Stephanie fastened her seat belt. "That would be the best route to take."

Isabella turned the key in the ignition, glanced over her left shoulder, then pulled away from the curb. A responsible driver—at least when her grandmother was in the car—she drove slowly through a neighborhood filled with large trees, green lawns, and two-story homes, most of them seventy or more years old.

"Who's this friend of yours, Grandma?"

"His name is James Scott. We went to school together when we were children."

"The name doesn't sound familiar. Do I know him?"

"No. James left Hart's Crossing a year before I married your grandfather."

Isabella cast her a surprised glance. "He's been gone *that* long? What made him come back here of all places?"

"He felt it's where God wants him."

Isabella didn't respond to that, and Stephanie didn't expect her to. She knew her granddaughter was going through a questioning phase, wondering as she began her senior year in high school what God wanted her to do with her future. She supposed Isabella would be surprised to learn the elderly also pray for God to show them what to do with their lives.

A few minutes later, they pulled to a stop near the curb in front of the house at 2240 Horizon Street.

As they stopped, Stephanie recalled another time when she'd sat in a car in front of the Scott home. It was a sunny day, much like this one, only in the spring. Instead of a midsize Subaru, that car was a 1948 Chevrolet Fleetmaster, better known as a "Woody." And unlike today, Stephanie hadn't been happy.

"You didn't have to join the army, Jimmy," Stephanie had whispered as she choked back tears. "What about college?"

"That's why I joined, Steph. It'll help pay for college when I get out. You know Mom can't afford to send me, and since I didn't get that football scholarship, this is the only way I can get to college."

"But what if you're sent to Korea?"

He put his arm around her shoulders. "I probably will be, honey. But I'll be okay. I don't plan to get hurt." He gave her a cocky grin.

Stephanie wanted to hit him. "Nobody *plans* to get hurt, Jimmy. Sometimes it just happens. Sometimes soldiers die." Right then, she felt like she might die, too.

"Hey. You know me. I'm tough. And I've got to come back for my best girl, don't I?"

She let her tears fall then, crying her heart out, and Jimmy held her close as he promised again and again that he would be okay.

He'd been right about that. James hadn't been injured in Korea. But neither had he returned to Hart's Crossing for Stephanie. By the time he got out of the military, things had changed for them both.

Stephanie couldn't help thinking that life was made more interesting by the different twists and turns it took along the way.

The door to the screened-in porch opened, and James stepped into view. He waved at her, then came down the four steps and walked briskly toward the car.

Stephanie pressed the button to lower her window. "Hello, James. Isn't it a beautiful day?"

"It certainly is." He opened the rear door and folded himself into the compact area behind Stephanie.

"This is my granddaughter, Isabella. Isabella, this is Mr. Scott."

"Hey, Mr. Scott." Isabella put the car in gear.

"A pleasure to meet you, young lady. Thanks for the lift."

"Any time for a friend of my grandma."

"Isabella looks like you," James told Stephanie half an hour later as they sat, side by side, on the metal bleachers, with stadium seats supporting their backs.

Stephanie's smile told him she was pleased by his observation.

"And she's got that same charisma you had at that age."

That comment made her blush.

"Does your grandson look like you, too?"

She laughed, a pretty sound. "Heavens, no. He's the spitting image of his father. Only taller. Very tall for a boy his age. He turned sixteen this month."

"What position does he play?"

"Halfback. No, wait. Maybe he's a fullback. Oh, dear. I can never keep those positions straight. I was never much on football."

"I remember." And he did. Back when they were in school, she only went to the games because he was on the team, and even then, she went reluctantly. Stephanie had much preferred the theater arts and music to sports.

The high school band struck up a rousing chorus of the school song as it marched into view. It wasn't a large band, but the kids played with enthusiasm. Right after the band came the visiting team. Across the field, the fans of the Pioneers gave shouts of encouragement.

The noise level shot up several decibels when the Hornets, wearing the school colors of black and gold, ran onto the field. Parents and students jumped to their feet, cheering and waving signs, flags, and banners. The Hart's Crossing cheerleaders jumped and flipped and shook their pom-poms.

"Which one is your grandson?" James shouted above the din.

Stephanie hesitated a moment, her gaze moving down the line of players who stood on the opposite side of the field. Then she pointed. "There he is. Number 32."

James squinted. His eyesight was good for a man his age, but the width of a football field made reading the numbers on the football jerseys a challenge. When he finally found the boy, he nodded. "You're right. He is a tall drink of water."

She beamed with a grandmother's pride, and James couldn't help thinking she was the prettiest woman in the stadium.

CHAPTER FOUR

For more than two decades, James and Martha Scott had attended a thriving interdenominational church on the east side of Puget Sound. The last James heard, the membership had grown to well over three thousand.

Back when his wife's health began to fail and the long drive to church each Sunday became impossible, members of the congregation had come to them, bringing love, comfort, prayers, and meals. And they'd kept coming, through the long days and weeks and months of her illness and the many hospitalizations, through her death and the funeral, through James's time of mourning.

Leaving that godly family had been the most difficult part of his move from Washington.

As the congregation of Hart's Crossing Community Church sang the last stanza of "O for a Thousand Tongues to Sing," James couldn't help thinking what a contrast this much smaller body of believers was to his former church. Yet the same Spirit was unmistakably present here. What an awesome thing that was, to know, no matter where he went, that the Lord would be there before him.

While he missed the electric keyboard, guitars, drums, and contemporary music of his former church—a surprising admission, perhaps, for a man of his age—James found no fault with the sermon delivered by John Gunn. The pastor's teaching from the book of Romans was direct and passionate. James knew he'd be glad to hear this young man preach many a sermon.

He glanced at Stephanie, seated on his right. She looked lovely in that blue and white outfit of hers. Very becoming.

Till Hart was the one who'd invited James to come to Hart's Crossing Community this morning. When he arrived at the church, he looked around the sanctuary for her but didn't find her. Seeing Stephanie, it seemed a natural choice to sit beside her.

And why shouldn't he feel that way? They were friends. Longtime friends.

After another hymn and a benediction, the service ended. The sanctuary grew noisy, people visiting with one another as they dispersed.

John Gunn strode to the end of the pew where James stood. "You must be Mr. Scott." He held out a hand of welcome.

"Guilty as charged."

"Miss Hart told us you might visit today. We hope you'll return."

"I will. It was a good service."

The pastor motioned to an attractive woman on the opposite side of the sanctuary. As she drew closer, he confirmed what James suspected. "This is my wife, Anne Gunn. Anne, I'd like you to meet James Scott. He grew up in Hart's Crossing but has lived in Washington for many years. Isn't that what I heard? Washington State."

"Yes, that's right. In the Seattle area."

Anne shook his hand as her husband had moments before. "Welcome, Mr. Scott."

"Thanks. It's good to be here."

They visited for a few minutes until James sensed Stephanie moving away from him toward the opposite end of the pew. As politely and quickly as he could, he brought the conversation with John and Anne Gunn to a close with a promise to return the next Sunday. Then he retrieved his well-worn Bible from the pew and followed after Stephanie.

He caught up with her outside. "Steph."

She turned toward him.

Until that moment, he hadn't known what he intended to say. "I was wondering if you might have lunch with me. We could drive up to the resort, if you'd like. It would be my way of thanking you for the delightful time I had yesterday at the game."

She hesitated a moment before she gave her head a slow shake. "I'm sorry, James. My lunch is already cooking in the crock-pot."

"Oh." He was surprised by the disappointment her refusal caused. "Well, another time then."

She touched his forearm with her fingertips before he could move away. "Perhaps you'd like to join me at my place. The food won't be as fancy as what the lodge at Timber Creek serves, but it's nutritious."

His disappointment was gone in a flash. "If you're sure I wouldn't be intruding."

"I wouldn't have asked if that were the case." Her smile was as light and lovely as the Indian summer day.

James's old ticker beat like a set of bongos. "Then I'll be glad to come. When should I be there?"

"You may come now, if you like."

He would like. He would like it a lot.

The pot roast and vegetables that simmered in the crock-pot would normally provide four meals for Stephanie. But men usually had bigger appetites, James included if that Scarecrow burger he'd devoured on Friday was any indication.

"Please make yourself at home," she told him as they entered her house. "I'll just be a few minutes."

She went into her bedroom and changed from her Sunday attire into a pink cotton blouse and a pair of comfortable denim slacks. A quick glance at the full length mirror told her she'd added a few pounds over the summer. She would have to do something about that. Why did weight maintenance become so difficult as one grew older?

Never mind. Diets were best begun on Mondays. This was Sunday, and she had a guest waiting for her in the living room.

Not just any guest either. An old friend, one who was feeling lonely after his return to his hometown. She'd seen his loneliness in his eyes when she declined his invitation to dine at the resort. That was why she'd asked him to join her here. One old friend helping another.

"Can I get you anything to drink?" she called to James on her way to the kitchen.

"No, thanks." He appeared in the doorway. "I'd like to help. Why don't I set the table?"

There was something special, something intimate, about his offer, and her heart fluttered in response. "Okay." She motioned toward the sideboard. "You'll find napkins and the silverware in there."

"I like the way you've decorated the kitchen. This pale shade of green is very restful on the eyes."

Stephanie laughed softly as she lifted the lid of the crock-pot.

"What?"

She glanced over her shoulder, meeting his gaze. "Oh, I just thought of how Chuck wouldn't have noticed if I'd painted the walls with red and white stripes. He could be terribly obtuse at times." Odd, the way some things that were irritating about a loved one when they were with you became the very things you missed the most after they were gone.

Unexpected tears stung her eyes, and she glanced away, not wanting James to see them.

There was tender understanding in his voice as he said, "We're two lucky people, you and I. We both had good, long marriages."

Stephanie wiped her eyes with the hem of her apron. "I don't believe in luck. Making a marriage last fifty years takes God's blessing, plenty of faith and love, and even more grit and determination." She turned and offered James a tremulous smile. "But you know that as well as I do."

He nodded. "Yes, I do."

James returned to his table-setting duties. Stephanie suspected he was giving her time to collect her emotions, and she was grateful.

A short while later, with their food on the table, James pulled out a chair for her.

"Thank you, James."

"My pleasure. And I'm the one who needs to say thanks. This is much nicer than eating by myself." He sat opposite her.

"Would you like to say the blessing?"

"I'd be honored." He bowed his head.

Stephanie listened to his prayer and, when he was done, echoed his amen. Eyes open again, she motioned toward the platter of food in the center of the small kitchen table. "Please. Help yourself."

As he did so, he said, "Pastor Gunn preached an excellent sermon this morning."

"He's a gifted teacher. We're fortunate to have him. Although I must admit I wasn't so sure when he first came to us. He's so young. Not yet forty."

James chuckled. "Amazing, isn't it? How forty became young. Remember the sixties when it was 'don't trust anyone over thirty.' I'm thinking eighty looks pretty good these days."

She nodded. It was true. In her mind, she was young, still ready and able to conquer the world. Her body, however, was headed downhill fast. There were times when she caught a glimpse of her reflection in the mirror and wondered who it was. Not her, certainly.

"Steph, I'm curious about something. Do you ever regret not leaving Hart's Crossing?"

She pondered the question, testing her feelings. "No. Not really. I've always been happy here. There are drawbacks to small town life, of course, but there are advantages, too. We know our next-door neighbors, and we never have to fight rush-hour traffic. Chuck had a good job with the county highway district. They hired him in 1955, and he worked there until he retired. Not many people stay with the same company for that long these days."

"No, indeed."

"At least twice a year, Chuck took me to Boise or Salt Lake for the weekend so we could see a play or the opera. He called it my biannual culture fix. Once he took me to New York City for an entire week. We saw five Broadway shows. It was heaven."

"You always were passionate about the theater."

She felt a rush of pleasure that James remembered that about her.

"You were a good actress, too. I wouldn't have been surprised to learn you were a famous performer on Broadway or a movie star."

Stephanie laughed softly, denying his comment with a shake of her head, even though acting on Broadway had been her dream, once upon a time and long, long ago.

James's gaze was gentle, and although he didn't laugh aloud, she knew he enjoyed the shared memories as much as she did. Then, ever so slowly, his smile faded. His eyes narrowed, and his brows drew together in concentration.

After a long silence, he said, "Sometimes I wonder what would've happened to us if I hadn't joined the army."

Stephanie's heart skipped a beat, for James's question mirrored her own thoughts. Her own *guilty* thoughts. It seemed wrong for them to sit in this kitchen, in a home her husband had paid for, wondering what might have been between them if James hadn't left Hart's Crossing.

And still she wondered.

CHAPTER FIVE

From: "James Scott" <jtscott@fiberpipe.net>
Sent: Wednesday, September 28 8:02 AM
To: "Jenna & Ray" <jscottengland@yahoo.com>
Subject: Greetings from Idaho

Hello, Jenna and Ray.

All is well here. You'll be pleased to know
that I feel more settled in my new/old home.
The boxes are dwindling away a few more each
day. It's amazing how many things your mother
and I accumulated over the years. I sold a lot
in my garage sale but maybe not enough. Don't
worry. I did keep everything you said you
wanted, and those things are in boxes in my
garage.

Jenna, I know you were worried about me
moving to this small town after being gone
for five decades, but I can assure you, I'm
going to be quite happy. The slower pace of
Hart's Crossing agrees with me. Many of the
people I knew as a boy have either moved or
passed away, but there are a few old friends
who still live here. It's good to become
reacquainted with them.

I attended a small community church on Sunday
and feel certain it will become my church
home. The pastor is a young man—in his late
thirties, I think—and an excellent teacher.
He's on fire for the Lord, which is something
I want in a pastor. You know how important it
is for your father to be planted in a good,
Bible-believing church. I can do without a
lot, but I can't do without that. Or I sure
wouldn't want to do without it, at any rate.

After church, I dined at the home of one of
those old friends I mentioned above. I was
one grade ahead of Stephanie Watson when we
were in school. (Her last name was Carlson
then.) She's a lovely woman. You would like
her. She was widowed last year. She and her
husband were married even longer than your
mother and I.

I've hired a neighbor boy to mow the yard
every week, and come spring, I'm going to get
the exterior of the house painted. I'm not

too fond of the bright shade of blue that's on there now.

By the time you two come to visit me, I should have a guest room all ready for you. I hope that visit will be some time soon. I miss you.

Love, Dad

P.S. My new phone number is 208-555-4632. I haven't changed my cellular service yet, and I still don't have an answering machine hooked up. Best time to catch me at home is in the morning.

From:	"Jenna Scott-Kirkpatrick"
	<jscottengland@yahoo.com>
Sent:	Wednesday, September 21 10:02 PM
To:	"Dad" <jtscott@fiberpipe.net>
Subject:	Glad all is well

Hi, Daddy. Your email was waiting for me when I got home from work. I'm glad to know you're doing okay. I still don't understand why you wanted to move to Idaho, but it sounds like, for now, you're glad that you did. Just remember, you can always go back to Washington. Nobody will blame you if you change your mind.

Ray and I are planning a holiday in Greece
within the next twelve months. He isn't sure
when he'll be able to take his vacation, so we
have to be flexible. Who knows when we'll make
it back to the States? You should get your
passport in order and come see us.

I'm glad to know you're making friends,
but please be careful when it comes to
relationships with lonely widows. You're a
handsome man who's financially well off. Some
women would be eager to take advantage of you,
you know. Don't lose your head, Daddy.

I love you,

Jenna

"Don't lose my head," James muttered, staring at
the computer screen. "Women eager to take advantage
of me. Of all the idiotic—" He cut himself off before
he said or thought something he would regret.

Why did Jenna insist on treating him like a half-
wit? No, worse than that. Like a child. Imagine what
Jenna would have written if she knew he and Stephanie
were going to the movies tomorrow evening.

He took several long, calming breaths.

In his daughter's defense, Jenna had no way of knowing what a wonderful woman Stephanie was. But he still thought it best if he didn't mention his growing attraction for Stephanie Watson in future emails to his children.

"What they don't know can't hurt them."

James glanced through the remainder of the email in the Inbox. Nothing from either Kurt or Paula, but there was the daily devotional from purposedrivenlife. com. He paused to read it, and his spirits lifted in response to the words on the screen. It was good to know, even at the ripe old age of seventy, that God still had a purpose for his life.

Speaking of purpose, he'd best get on with his day. He closed the email program and powered down the computer.

A short while later, he backed his late-model Buick LeSabre out of the garage and drove to Smith's Market. For a small grocery store, the selection of packaged items and fresh foods was reasonably good. James wasn't picky at any rate. One of the downsides of growing older was the diminished delight one had in eating good food. Martha had been a gourmet cook, so James knew something about fine dining. Those days were gone.

Well, he supposed the lessened enjoyment helped keep his weight down, so he should be grateful.

He pushed the shopping cart around the end of the aisle and stopped when he saw Stephanie placing a box of Grape-Nuts into the red shopping basket on her left arm.

Now here was something he could still enjoy, he thought. Just seeing her brought a smile to his heart.

What would *have happened between us if I hadn't joined the army?* The question had plagued him since Sunday. And now, as he looked at her in this grocery aisle, new questions joined the first. *Would we have gotten married? Would we have had kids together? Would we have been happy?*

She glanced up. "James." A pale blush pinkened her cheeks.

"Good morning, Steph."

They hadn't seen one another since he went to her home for dinner, although they'd spoken by telephone when he called to ask her to the movies. Now he was keenly aware of how much he'd wanted to see her again.

"Good morning," she replied. "Doing a bit of shopping, I see."

He glanced down at the items in his cart, then up again. "Nothing that'll taste as delicious as the meal we shared."

The color in her cheeks intensified. That was the moment he suspected she'd thought of him often this week, too.

Will wonders never cease.

Oh, Jenna wouldn't be happy about this development. She wouldn't be happy at all.

The Apollo Theater first opened its doors in May of 1927. The premier attraction was *Don Juan* starring John Barrymore.

In the years that followed, the theater saw the townsfolk of Hart's Crossing through the Great Depression, through World War II, through the turbulent sixties, through good times and bad times and everything in between. In the eighties, the theater doors closed, and folks expected the building would be torn down. But then Dave Coble, the town's current chief of police, bought the theater and began a lengthy period of historical restoration and modern improvements.

The Apollo's grand reopening occurred in late 1995. *Toy Story* was the feature film that weekend. Some people in town saw the movie two and three times.

One of Stephanie's earliest memories was of coming to the Apollo with her parents, her father wearing a suit and fedora, her mother in a floral print dress, hat, and gloves. Stephanie couldn't have been more than four years old at the time, but she remembered sitting in the first row of the balcony. She could still recall the images of horses galloping across the screen.

Another of her memories closely associated with the Apollo was of her first kiss. It was *that* memory that replayed in her mind as she and James approached the ticket booth on Friday evening.

"I hope it's a good film," James said.

"It's supposed to be excellent. I read a review in *People* when I was at the hair salon."

Friday wasn't her usual day to have her hair done, but she couldn't go to the movies with James with it looking a fright. So the instant the ladies of the Thimbleberry Quilting Club departed through the front door of her home this morning, Stephanie had hurried out the back door, into her car, and off to Terri's Tangles to get a cut and style.

James purchased two senior citizen tickets from the bored-looking teenager seated in the booth. When he turned toward Stephanie, her gaze slid to his lips, and she wondered what it would be like to kiss James now that he was a mature man.

Oh, what a thought! She never should have agreed to come with James tonight. This felt too much like a date. Dating? At her age? How ridiculous.

An odd smile curved the corners of James's mouth, as if he'd read her mind and was amused by what he found there.

Oh, good grief. She felt as giddy as a schoolgirl. Whatever on earth was wrong with her? She wasn't the giddy sort.

Tell that to the butterflies in her stomach.

"Would you like something from the snack bar?" James asked. "I could get us each a drink, and we could share a box of popcorn."

"All right." She doubted she could eat a single bite. "I'll have a Diet Coke, please."

While James stood in line for their refreshments, Stephanie waited in the lobby near the entrance to the theater. She studied the various posters on the walls that advertised the movies coming to the Apollo in weeks to come. During the school year, the theater was only open on the weekends, Friday evening through the Sunday matinee. Most movies played for one weekend, the occasional blockbuster being the exception to that rule.

There weren't many people here tonight, which caused her to wonder about the review she'd read. Maybe the film wasn't good after all. But she supposed the high school kids came to the 9:00 show.

She turned her head and saw Liz Rue, owner of the Tattered Pages Bookstore, walking toward her. "Hi, Steph. I'm glad I ran into you. The book you ordered came in today. I meant to call you, but I kept getting interrupted."

"That's all right. I wasn't in any rush. I'll come into the bookstore tomorrow to get it."

"Say, would you like to sit with Ivan and me? It's no fun to go to the movies alone and we—"

James stepped to Stephanie's side, holding a cardboard tray with the two large drinks and a large popcorn in it. "Sorry that took so long."

Liz looked as if she were choking on her unfinished sentence.

"Liz, have you met James Scott? James, this is Liz Rue. She owns the bookstore on Main Street, across from the Good Buy Market."

James nodded his head to acknowledge the introduction. "Nice to meet you, Ms. Rue. I stopped in your store the other day. The Tattered Pages, right?"

"Yes." Liz's gaze moved from James to Steph to James again.

Was she surprised to see Stephanie out with a man? Or was it seeing her with this particular man—the one who bore a striking resemblance to *People*'s Sexiest Man Alive—that surprised her more? Whichever it was, Stephanie had a sinking feeling she and James were about to become grist for the rumor mill.

How embarrassing!

James said, "Steph, let's find our seats, shall we?" To Liz, he added, "Please excuse us, Ms. Rue. I don't like to miss the previews of coming attractions."

"Of course. Enjoy the show. Steph, don't forget to pick up that book."

"I won't."

Longing for the dim light of the theater to hide her flushed cheeks, Stephanie followed James. He motioned her into a row, and she sank onto the second seat off the aisle, wishing she could simply disappear.

As James handed her the Diet Coke, he leaned close and whispered, "I don't mind, you know."

She looked at him, but his eyes were hidden in shadows. "Mind what?"

"I don't mind if they gossip about us." He paused, and she could just make out his smile. "Not if what they're saying is true."

Slowly, hesitantly, he leaned over and pressed his lips against her right cheek.

CHAPTER SIX

Stephanie's dreams were filled with James and that gentle, sweet kiss he'd placed upon her cheek in the darkened movie theater. She awakened the next morning feeling gloriously, joyously alive.

Miranda arrived on her doorstep at 8:00 a.m.

"Well, this is a surprise."

Judging by her daughter's dour expression, something was troubling her, but Stephanie didn't ask what. She'd learned through the years that it was best to let Miranda open up on her own.

She motioned her daughter inside, then led the way into the kitchen. "I didn't expect to see you today. I thought Foster had an away game."

"He does. We'll leave town in a little bit. I came over while Vince packs the car."

"Coffee?"

Her daughter shook her head. "No, thanks."

Stephanie poured herself a cup.

"Mom, are you okay?" Miranda leaned her shoulder against the refrigerator.

"I'm fine." She turned from the coffeemaker. "Why do you ask?"

"I don't know. I just thought . . . Well, maybe I haven't been paying enough attention to you lately. I know you must get lonely, with Dad gone."

Stephanie nodded. "Yes, sometimes I'm lonely. But it's all right. I know you all have busy lives. I remember what it was like when you were in high school and going several directions at once. And I wasn't juggling a job like you are. I don't expect you to be at my beck and call, dear."

Miranda worried her lower lip, a frown furrowing her brow.

"Oh my," Stephanie said softly, realizing at last the reason for her daughter's unexpected visit.

"What?"

"This is about my date with James last night, isn't it?"

"Your *date?*" Miranda straightened away from the refrigerator.

Ironic, wasn't it? To have her daughter objecting to that term. Stephanie had resisted it, too—up until the moment last night when James kissed her.

Quelling a smile, Stephanie said, "Isn't that what they still call it when a man and woman go out to the movies?" She carried her coffee to the kitchen table and sat down.

"Mom, this isn't like you."

"What isn't like me, honey?" She feigned ignorance. Or innocence. Or both.

Was it wicked to tease her daughter this way?

Miranda joined her at the table. "Isabella says that man is an old school friend of yours. I'm sorry I didn't meet him last weekend. I should have been at the game, but—"

"His name is James." Stephanie felt a warm glow just saying it. "James Scott."

"Whatever. James. Fine." Her daughter was getting more distraught with every word. "But, Mom, you don't know anything about him. He hasn't lived here in, what? Fifty years?"

She couldn't contain the smile a moment longer. "Fifty-two."

"You shouldn't rush into a relationship, Mom."

Her good humor began to fade. "I would hardly call going to a movie rushing into a relationship. And you're wrong about my not knowing anything about James. You'd be surprised by the number of subjects we've talked about in a short period of time. He's articulate and he's interesting and he's got a delightful sense of humor."

"But people in town are *talking*, Mom."

"Then let them talk." Stephanie squeezed her coffee cup between both hands. Last week, she'd felt guilty for enjoying his company. Last night, she'd been embarrassed when she realized others might gossip about her and James. But this morning, everything was different.

"Unless I'm breaking the law or falling into sin, what I do is no one's business but mine."

"*Mo-o-o-om.*" Her daughter drew the word out in a wheedling tone.

"And it isn't *your* business either, dear."

Miranda drew back in surprise.

Trying to soften her rebuke, Stephanie said, "I'm a grown woman, Miranda. I know my own mind and heart." She took a sip of coffee, giving herself a moment to weigh her words. "I may be a senior citizen, but I don't have one foot in the grave. I have every intention of living as full a life as the Lord will allow in the time I have left on earth. Your grandmother lived to be ninety-two, and her mother lived to be ninety-five. If I inherited those same genes, I may have another twenty-five years in me." She leaned forward. "How would you want me to spend those years?"

"I . . . You . . ." Miranda glanced at her wristwatch. "Oh, great. I've got to go." She rose. "We'll talk about this another time."

Stephanie gave her daughter a patient smile. "If you wish."

A few moments later, alone again, Stephanie released a deep sigh. Had she been unkind or unreasonable in what she said to Miranda? She hoped not.

Lord, show me if I was in the wrong. She's my daughter and she cares about me. I don't want to hurt her.

She sipped her cooling coffee.

Is it wrong for me to feel such fondness for James? Is it wrong for me to want to be with him? Am I being a foolish old woman?

Perhaps she was reading too much into that simple kiss. James hadn't held her hand during the movie or tried to kiss her again after he took her home. Perhaps they were friends and nothing more.

Do I want it to be something more?

"Yes," she whispered, her heart acknowledging the admission with its quickened beat. "Yes, I think I do."

The Scott family photograph album lay open on the coffee table. It was a thick book, lovingly assembled by Martha through the decades. The cover had changed several times, as had the type of binding. At first, it had been a simple affair. But after his wife took a scrapbooking class about a decade or so ago, the album had become a work of art, beautifully detailing the years of their marriage. James and Martha's wedding day. The births of each of their children. Vacations at the shore. Countless firsts—first teeth, first steps, first days of school, first home, first brand-new, not-previously-owned automobile. Photographs of the children graduating from high school, then college. Photographs of the children's weddings. Photographs of the grandchildren.

James flipped slowly through the pages that chronicled forty-seven years of his life. Sometimes he smiled. Once or twice he wiped away a tear. Always he remembered and was grateful.

When Martha died, James thought this album was complete, but of course, it wasn't. Nor should it be. Another chapter of the story was finished. That was all. Just a chapter. Not the book.

The two weeks since he'd arrived in Hart's Crossing had proved that.

And today he'd discovered something new: James Scott was in love. Unexpectedly, completely in love with Stephanie Carlson Watson, his childhood sweetheart. After a fifty-two-year detour, his heart had returned to that first, innocent love of his youth.

Who would have imagined that was possible? Not James. His marriage to Martha had been a happy one. They'd had their ups and downs, of course. He and Martha had been known to fight with passion. They'd made up the same way. But love—or lack of it—had never been an issue. He'd never been tempted to be unfaithful. Never.

He toyed with that thought a moment. Was he being unfaithful to Martha by falling in love with Stephanie?

No, his heart answered with confidence. He even thought Martha would be pleased, were it possible for her to look down from heaven and see him today, because she'd been one of the most unselfish, truly giving people James had ever known.

Somehow he doubted his children, especially Jenna, would see it that way.

He closed the album, then covered his face with his hands, his elbows resting on his thighs.

Lord, I'm in love with Steph, and I want to spend what years I can with her. I've got the feeling that's why you brought me back to Hart's Crossing. So unless you show me otherwise, I'm going to ask her to marry me.

He ran his fingers through his gray hair.

And Lord, I haven't proposed to a girl since I was a G.I. Just a kid. This time, I'm going to need your help and lots of it.

CHAPTER SEVEN

The first Sunday that James had visited Hart's Crossing Community Church, he'd come alone. He'd sat beside Stephanie because she was the first person he saw whom he knew. The next Sunday—the one following their night at the Apollo—he'd come alone but looked for her and only her.

This Sunday was a different story. He'd arranged to escort Stephanie to church, after which the two of them would drive to the resort located in the mountains north of Hart's Crossing. At the Timber Creek Lodge, they would enjoy a sumptuous dinner prepared by a French chef of some renown.

What happened after that would be up to Stephanie.

James had a hard time concentrating on the sermon, and even singing one of his favorite hymns, "Rock of Ages," didn't help the nerves twisting in his belly. He was mightily relieved to hear the benediction spoken. He hoped Stephanie wouldn't be prone to linger and visit.

She must have read his mind. While she was polite, nodding her head and saying good morning to this friend and that, she didn't allow anyone to delay their departure. In short order, they were seated in James's Buick and driving out of town.

Once they reached the highway and a cruising speed of fifty-five, James said, "I have some worship music CDs in the player. Instrumentals. No singing. Would you like to hear them?"

"That would be lovely."

He pushed a button, and the soft sounds of stringed instruments came through the speakers.

James cleared his throat, feeling the need for conversation. "I was hoping your daughter would be in church this morning. I've wanted to meet her."

"Miranda and her family attend the Baptist church over on Park Street. Didn't I tell you that?"

Maybe she had. They'd talked about many things—their children, their grandchildren, his career, her hobbies, the Bible, sports, people they'd known as children in Hart's Crossing, and so much more.

"When Miranda got married, she wanted to establish a life separate from her father and me, and that included going to a different church. She feared that too many people would still think of her as Stephanie and Chuck's daughter rather than as an adult. She wanted to make her own traditions and not feel as if she was still tied to her mother's apron strings." She paused briefly, then added, "Not that she *was* tied to them. Miranda was always fiercely independent, even as a toddler."

"Sounds like my Jenna." James laughed softly. "The word *independent* doesn't begin to describe her. For a long time, her mother and I doubted she would give up her precious autonomy for a more traditional lifestyle of love and marriage. But when she was thirty-six, she met Ray, and she fell for him. Hard." *A lot like her dad at the age of seventy.* "They were married just a few months later."

"Love is a wonderful thing."

James glanced quickly to his right, then back at the road. "Yes."

"You and I were very blessed to find the partners we did."

"Yes."

"So few people have staying power these days." She sighed. "At the first sign of trouble, they're ready to pack their bags and look for someone else to make them happy. They forget that love is an act of will as well as an emotion."

Music floated on the air as both driver and passenger became lost in thought.

As the Buick followed the highway into the mountains, twisting and weaving as it climbed to a higher elevation, the question James had asked at their first Sunday dinner replayed once again in Stephanie's mind.

"Sometimes I wonder what would've happened to us if I hadn't joined the army."

They would have married, Stephanie answered silently. They would have married and had children and grown old together. But God had taken them in different directions. God had given them different partners to love and cherish, and that had been good and right.

But now? Now here they were, without Martha, without Chuck, still alive and still wanting to love and be loved. Was it possible that what might have been could happen yet?

James *had* kissed her on that Friday night, after all. And in these past weeks, they'd talked and talked and talked, in person and by telephone. They'd taken long walks together. They'd sat on his porch in the warmth of the afternoon while he read poetry aloud from a book with worn covers. They'd cooked for each other, and they'd eaten together at the diner. And they'd talked and talked and talked.

But was she reading more into all of it than was there? He hadn't attempted to kiss her again. Perhaps he was just lonely after moving away from all his friends in Washington, from the home where he'd raised his family. That kiss, after all, had been on her cheek rather than the lips.

Goodness. Was she being a foolish old woman?

Chuck had teased her unmercifully about her romantic imagination and her fondness for three-hanky movies and novels. Was that what she was doing now? Letting her romantic imagination run wild?

Oh, dear.

"Look at all of that new development!" James exclaimed.

Pulled from her anxious thoughts, Stephanie looked at James instead of out the window.

"I had no idea things had changed this much up here," he said. "Some of those homes are enormous. Who can afford mansions around here?"

"Californians. Movie stars." Now Stephanie turned to gaze at the passing terrain and the elegant homes built along Timber Creek. "Most of these are vacation homes. The owners come here to ski in the winter or ride horses in the summer."

"I had no idea."

82

Stephanie wondered if he would be equally surprised to learn how her feelings for him had changed. Would it frighten him to know that she might care for him as more than a friend? That she might be . . . falling in love with him for the second time in her life?

Oh, dear. Oh, dear.

The dining room at the Timber Creek Lodge was large with high ceilings and an enormous stone fireplace as its focal point. Plate glass windows faced the main chair lift, and in the winter, diners could watch skiers and snowboarders *shooshing* down the mountainside. But now, in early autumn, the mountains were free of snow. Instead of a blanket of white on the ground, the changing colors of the trees provided a visual smorgasbord of orange, yellow, and red.

Since this was the off-season for the resort, the dining room wasn't busy when James and Stephanie arrived shortly after 12:30. The hostess led them to a table for two near the window. Their eyes were protected from the bright October sunshine by a wide awning.

"How beautiful," Stephanie said as she sat on the chair James held for her.

He didn't take his eyes off her. "Very beautiful."

"Your server will be Brandilyn," the hostess said. She set the menus on the table. "She'll be right with you."

"Thank you." James sat on the chair opposite Stephanie.

She looked at him. "I haven't been here in years. Thank you for bringing me. I'd forgotten what a lovely place this is."

"You don't ski anymore?"

"At my age?"

"You're not too old to ski. I still go several times each winter."

"I haven't skied since high school. I never liked it much."

"You didn't?" He was genuinely surprised. "But you came up here with me a lot."

"You're right. I did." A soft smile curved her mouth. "I guess it was the company that made it fun."

Encouraged by her words, James decided he couldn't wait until after they'd eaten. He had to say what he felt or burst. "I've always enjoyed the pleasure of your company. You know that."

There was that attractive splash of pink in her cheeks again.

"Steph, I'd like—" He swallowed hard, took a quick breath, then began again. "I'd like to have the pleasure of your company for the rest of my days."

Her eyes widened.

Lord, have I gone too fast? Did I make a mistake? Am I going to blow this?

He drew another breath and hurried on. "If I were a young man with what seems like all the time in the world, I'd wait to tell you what I'm feeling and thinking. I'd wait until I was certain what your answer would be. But I'm no longer young. Neither of us are. We both understand how quickly life rushes by." He reached into his jacket pocket. "I love you, Steph Watson. I've lived long enough to understand what it is I'm feeling. I want to be with you for the rest of my life." He pushed the small box across the table. "I love you, and I'm asking you to do me the honor of becoming my wife."

"Oh my," she whispered.

Was that a good *oh-my* or a bad *oh-my*?

She opened the lid of the small white box. "Oh, James. I—"

"It was my mother's ring. It'll probably need to be resized. And if you prefer to have a wedding ring you pick out yourself, we can—"

"It's a beautiful ring, James." She sniffed softly. "Beautiful."

"Steph, is there any chance you might—"

She looked up. "Yes."

Yes, what?

"Yes, I'll be your wife." She brushed away tears with her knuckles. "I love you, too."

He was afraid to believe she'd given the answer he wanted. "Are you sure? I mean, you don't need some time to pray about it?"

"I'm sure." She laughed through her tears. "I've been talking to the Lord about you for days."

His spirits rose to new heights. "My kids will think we're crazy. They'll think we're moving too fast."

"So will Miranda."

As if prompted by an unseen director, they leaned forward. Their lips met above the center of the table.

The kiss might have lasted longer if their waitress hadn't arrived, making a throat-clearing sound to get their attention.

Unabashed, James looked at the waitress and said, "Congratulate us, miss. This lovely woman has agreed to marry me."

CHAPTER EIGHT

From: "James Scott" <jtscott@fiberpipe.net>
Sent: Monday, October 10 6:10 AM
To: "Kurt & Neta" <kurtscott@fiberpipe
             .net>; "Jenna & Ray"
             <jscottengland@yahoo.com>; "Paula"
             <carpoolmom@fiberpipe.net>
Subject: Glad tidings

Dear Kurt & Neta, Jenna & Ray, Paula, and all
my beloved grandchildren,

I've got some important news to share, and
I hope you'll rejoice with me. I've asked
Stephanie Watson, a dear, dear friend from my
boyhood, to be my wife, and she's agreed. I
could not be happier than I am today. As you
know, few men are fortunate to find one woman
who will love and cherish them, for better or

worse, richer or poorer, in sickness and in health—and *mean* it! I've been blessed to have it happen twice.

I know you'll think I'm rushing into this, but I assure you I haven't lost my faculties. Steph and I are mature enough to know our feelings, and we understand what marriage means, having both had long and loving marriages that ended with the deaths of our spouses.

I hope you'll also be reassured that we've prayed about this, before either of us knew what the other was feeling. I believe God brought me back to Hart's Crossing (at least partly) so that I might have this blessing in my latter years. I am truly a happy, happy man.

We haven't decided when the wedding will take place. By the end of October, we hope. Maybe early November. I know that isn't much time. Only a few weeks to plan. It would mean the world to have all of you present, but I'll understand if it isn't possible because of work and school. However, I'd be glad to check airline schedules and so forth, and I can cover some of the cost of the airfare if that will help get you here. Between Stephanie's home and my home, there is room for everybody, even if some would have to sleep on blow-up mattresses on the floor. Let me know if you can come.

I love you all,

Dad/Grandpa

From: "Jenna Scott-Kirkpatrick"
   <jscottengland@yahoo.com>
Sent: Monday, October 10 5:50 PM
To: "Dad" <jtscott@fiberpipe.net>; "Kurt
   Scott" <kurtscott@fiberpipe.net>;
   "Paula Scott" <carpoolmom@fiberpipe
   .net>
Subject: Re: Glad tidings

Daddy, you can't be serious about marrying
that woman this soon. You barely know her.
Please, stop and consider what you are
doing. I'm sure you'll discover this is just
loneliness. You never should have moved.
That's why you're having a crisis now.

I'll call you tomorrow. Please don't do
anything rash in the meantime.

Love, Jenna

From: "Kurt Scott" <kurtscott@fiberpipe
   .net>
Sent: Monday, October 10 6:22 PM
To: "James Scott" <jtscott@fiberpipe
   .net>; "Jenna Scott-Kirkpatrick"

                <jscottengland@yahoo.com>; "Paula
                Scott" <carpoolmom@fiberpipe.net>
Subject: Re: Glad tidings

Hi, Dad. I don't know what to say. Are you
sure you know what you're doing? Of course,
Neta and I just want your happiness, but this
seems mighty quick for somebody who always
considered things from every angle before
making a decision.

Kurt

From: "Paula Scott" <carpoolmom@fiberpipe
              .net>
Sent: Monday, October 10 10:15 PM
To: "Dad" <jtscott@fiberpipe.net>; "Kurt"
              <kurtscott@fiberpipe.net>; "Jenna"
              <jscottengland@yahoo.com>
Subject: Re: Glad tidings

Oh, Dad. I'm thrilled for you. Forget what
Kurt and Jenna said. You just go right ahead
and be happy. When I get to work tomorrow,
I'll tell my supervisor that I need a week off
at the end of October or first of November.
You just let me know the date as quick as
you can. I'll try to use the frequent flyer
miles I've saved up, but I may need some help
with the tickets if there aren't any frequent

flyer seats to be had. One way or the other,
you can count on the girls and me being there
to celebrate with you and your bride. I can
hardly wait to meet Stephanie. I know we'll
love her, because you wouldn't love her if she
wasn't everything you say she is.

Love, Paula

Stephanie knocked on Miranda's front door and waited for an answer. There was a part of her that wished her daughter and family were out for the evening. Lucky James. He'd sent his children an email to announce their engagement.

"I suppose I should call each one of them," he'd told her, "but with their various work schedules and Jenna living overseas, this seems the better way."

The door opened, revealing Miranda.

"Mom." She paused. "This is a surprise."

An unpleasant surprise, judging by Miranda's tone. It was obvious her daughter hadn't forgiven her for what she'd said during their last conversation.

"I was hoping we could talk," Stephanie said.

"Sure. If you want. Come in. I was just finishing the supper dishes."

Miranda led the way into the kitchen. It was a large room with all the modern conveniences a person could imagine or wish for, designed for entertaining, although Miranda and Vince seldom entertained. For that matter, Miranda seldom cooked. She was the Schwan's deliveryman's best customer. Schwan's and Pizza Hut.

Oh, dear. She was being so critical of her daughter. The Bible instructed believers to take every thought captive for Christ, but Stephanie was failing miserably in that regard.

Miranda went to the dishwasher and continued loading it. Stephanie didn't wait for an invitation to sit on one of the kitchen chairs. It obviously wasn't going to come.

Sinking onto the seat cushion, Stephanie said, "I'm sorry if I hurt your feelings the other day. That wasn't my intent."

Another plate clattered into place on the lower rack.

"Miranda, I know you spoke out of concern for me."

"Yes, I did." Her daughter placed several glasses in the top rack.

Stephanie drew a deep breath, praying for courage. "I hope we'll be better able to handle what I have to tell you now."

Her daughter straightened. There was a look of dread in her eyes, as if she already suspected what her mother would say.

"James asked me to marry him, and I accepted."

"Mom!"

"I love him, Miranda. I want to be his wife."

"How can you say that?"

Stephanie rose from her chair. "Loving James doesn't mean I didn't love your father. Or that I don't still love him. He was my husband for fifty years. Most of the memories of my past are tied to him." She lifted a hand in supplication. "But, honey, James is my future. I want to make new memories with him."

Miranda dried her hands with a dish towel. "Do you know how outrageous this is? He's lived in Hart's Crossing . . . What? Three weeks? A month? And now you say you want to marry him. Mom, this isn't like you."

"Isn't it? Your father always said I was a hopeless romantic. I don't think he would be surprised . . . or disappointed. He'd be glad for me."

"If there's nothing wrong with this guy—" Miranda waved her hands in the air—"why haven't I met him yet?"

"It isn't as if I've been concealing him from you. I expected you two to meet the day of Foster's football game, but you never came."

"I got stuck at work. I told you that."

Stephanie pressed her lips together, swallowing the remark that the game was on a Saturday and nothing about her work in the mayor's office was so urgent it couldn't have waited a few hours. Besides, that wasn't what this visit to Miranda's was about.

Echoing Stephanie's thoughts, her daughter said, "That's beside the point. When *will* I meet him?"

Never seemed like a good answer. She and James could elope and go live on a deserted island somewhere in the South Pacific.

"Mom?"

It was difficult to tell from Miranda's tone if she was more angry or hurt. Stephanie didn't want her to be either.

"Come for supper tomorrow night. You, Vince, and the children. Shall we say 6:30?"

And please, God, soften her heart between now and then.

CHAPTER NINE

Early on Tuesday morning, James answered a knock on his back door. He felt a flash of pleasure at seeing Stephanie on the stoop. Then he saw the sadness in her eyes.

"Miranda didn't take it well," she said softly.

He drew her into the kitchen and into his arms.

"I don't understand why she objects so strenuously." Her words were muffled against his shirt.

He patted her back. "Would it help if I spoke to her?"

"We'll find out tonight." She pulled back from his embrace. "I've invited Miranda and her family to come to supper to meet you." She grimaced. "You're to be the main course, I'm afraid."

James chuckled. "I think I'll rather enjoy that."

"Oh, James. Why couldn't she just be happy for me? This past year has been difficult enough, learning to be alone. I'd never been alone before. Not ever. I went from my father's house to my husband's house. After Chuck died, I thought I would be alone for the remainder of my days." She touched his cheek with her fingertips, adding, "But now, there's you, and I want to be with you."

Silently, he led her to the chairs at the table. After they sat, he took hold of both her hands, squeezing gently.

Tears filled her eyes, then spilled over. "She's so angry. I don't understand why she's so angry."

"I've given this some thought, and my guess is she feels threatened by your love for me. She's afraid she might lose the memories of her father if you marry again. Maybe she's afraid she'll lose you, too." James wiped the tears from her cheeks with the pads of his thumbs. "Don't cry, love. It will work itself out." His smile was meant to encourage. "Our children didn't have much time to get used to the idea of us dating, and already we're engaged. Once they see us together, they'll know we're doing the right thing."

"I'm not so sure, James. Miranda's so adamantly against it."

"Let me show you something. Wait here." He rose from the chair and went to his office, where he printed a copy of his youngest daughter's email. Upon returning to the kitchen, he handed the slip of paper to Stephanie.

He waited to see her smile. He expected her to be glad that Paula planned to come for the wedding. But that wasn't the response he got.

"What did Kurt and Jenna say?" She met his gaze. "Did they react like Miranda?"

He shrugged. "Not angry. A little concerned is all. But they'll come around. So will Miranda."

"Maybe we shouldn't get married so soon." She pushed a stray curl back from her forehead. "Maybe we should wait awhile."

Wait? If any two people should understand that there was no guarantee of tomorrow, it was James and Stephanie. Both of them had lost their life partners too soon. Now they had a chance for happiness together. They'd prayed about this marriage, separately and together, and both believed it to be God's will. What was the purpose of waiting?

James took hold of Stephanie's hands for the second time. "Don't falter now, Steph. We love each other." He looked deep into her eyes, willing her to see everything he felt for her—the love, the desire, the delight. "Don't break this old man's heart." He kissed her, his lips lingering a long while before he drew back and whispered, "I couldn't bear to lose you now."

Stephanie knew her love for James was real. Love wasn't a commodity that ran out or was used up over time. No, the more one loved, the more love one had to give. It multiplied as it was spent. Loving James didn't negate the love she'd had for Chuck. If anything, it made that love seem even more special. Because she'd been happy with her husband for fifty years, it made her want to taste that happiness again with James.

She wished her daughter understood that.

Stephanie stayed with James for another hour. Little by little, his quiet confidence helped calm her jangled nerves.

She left his house, feeling better than when she arrived, and drove toward Smith's Market to purchase the food for that night's supper. She wanted the gathering to be special. The menu would include grilled steaks, baked potatoes with all the fixings, and a nice tossed salad. Oh, and strawberry cheesecake. Cheesecake was Miranda's favorite dessert.

But instead of turning left onto Hart Street, she turned right and drove several blocks before she realized she'd gone the wrong direction. When she stopped the car, meaning to turn it around, she discovered she was in front of Francine's home.

Perhaps this hadn't been an accident, the result of wandering thoughts. Perhaps she'd been drawn here for a purpose.

It was no secret in Hart's Crossing that Francine and her daughter, Angie, had been estranged for many years. But since this past spring, their troubles had been resolved. The two of them were close again.

Hoping to gain some wisdom, Stephanie got out of the car and walked to the front of the Hunter home.

When the door opened, she was greeted by Francine's warm smile. "Steph. What a nice surprise."

"I hope I haven't come at a bad time. It's early, I know."

"Never too early for a visit with a friend," Francine answered. "Come in. Would you care for some coffee or tea?"

Stephanie shook her head. "No. I'm fine, thanks." She was anything but fine. Otherwise, she would be at the market, looking over the packages of steaks.

"Let's sit in the living room. We can enjoy the fall colors outside while we chat." After both had settled onto chairs, Francine leaned forward and patted Stephanie's knee. "What's troubling you, dear friend? You look like the world is atop your shoulders."

"It's about . . . it's about James. We . . . he and I . . . James asked me to marry him."

Francine's face broke into an enormous grin. "Oh, Steph. That's wonderful! I take it you had the good sense to say yes."

She nodded.

Francine rose from her chair and embraced Stephanie. "I couldn't be happier for you. Have you shared the news with any of the other Thimbleberries?"

"No. Not yet."

"Well, we must do so at once. Oh, they'll all be delighted. This is such marvelous news. A wedding. I love weddings."

Stephanie touched Francine's forearm, afraid she might head for the telephone immediately. "That isn't why I came. At least, not entirely." She waited until her old friend sat again. "It's about Miranda."

A knowing look replaced Francine's excitement. "She doesn't approve?"

"No. She thinks I'm being reckless or thoughtless. Or both. And she's angry about it."

"I'm sorry."

Stephanie opened her purse to retrieve a tissue. "Frani, I don't want to lose my daughter's love. I don't want us to be separated by this. I thought . . . I thought maybe you could give me some advice. You and Angie have worked out your differences. Tell me what I can do to make matters better between us."

103

"You want my advice?" Francine leaned back in her chair, steepling her hands and touching her fingertips to her lips. After a lengthy silence, she lowered her hands and said, "Steph, I lost count of how many mistakes I made with Angie. In the end, only God could fix things between us, and that's the only real advice I feel qualified to give you. Turn it over to him. Once I was willing to let go of Angie and get out of the Lord's way, the miracle happened. When things were at their darkest, I clung to the promise in Joel that says, 'I will give you back what you lost to the stripping locusts.' Angie and I were stripped bare in our relationship, but the Lord restored us."

With a nod, Stephanie turned her head to look out the window. She and Miranda weren't estranged. Not as Francine and Angie had once been. True, they often saw things from different perspectives, but they rarely argued. They had a good relationship—or at least, she always thought they did.

Am I making a mountain out of a molehill? Will she stop being angry if I give her some time?

"Steph, why don't we pray about this together? I may not have an answer, but God does."

Stephanie agreed with a nod, thankful for the offer, and the two women joined hands and bowed their heads.

James could have cut the tension at supper that night with the proverbial knife. Miranda Andrews was painfully polite, but there was no mistaking her true feelings about her mother's engagement.

Stephanie's grandchildren, Isabella and Foster, managed to keep the conversation going for the first hour, talking about what was happening at school and where Isabella hoped to go to college after graduation. But once the meal was done, James decided he was tired of tiptoeing around the real reason for the get-together.

Pushing his dessert plate back from the edge of the table, he said, "Miranda, I'm glad we finally managed to meet. I'm sorry it didn't happen sooner." His glance swept around the table, pausing briefly on her husband and children before returning to her. "You've got a terrific family."

"Thank you." Miranda's smile was brittle.

"I understand that you're concerned your mother and I are rushing into marriage. I want to assure you, we're not."

Miranda lifted her chin, and her eyes sparked with anger. "How can you say that? You're a stranger here."

"Not to your mother, I'm not." He reached for Stephanie's hand. "We know each other—" with his free hand, he tapped his chest—"in here."

"You haven't seen each other more than a time or two in the past fifty years, Mr. Scott."

"Please call me James." He smiled, hoping to break through her defenses with a bit of humor. "I love your mother, and if I hadn't been so shy, I would've asked her to marry me even sooner."

The joke fell flat. If anything, Miranda looked appalled by his comment.

Vince, who'd said little throughout the meal, leaned toward his wife. "Honey, give the guy a chance. Hear what he has to say."

James didn't know who deserved his sympathies—Miranda, with her simmering hurt and anger; or her husband, for the glare his comment earned him; or their kids, who looked like two deer caught in the headlights, longing to escape.

Stephanie apparently felt the most sorry for her grandchildren. "Isabella, why don't you and Foster take these dishes into the kitchen?"

"Sure, Grandma."

The adults said nothing more until the grateful teenagers escaped from the dining room.

James glanced at Stephanie and gave her fingers a squeeze before turning his gaze on Miranda once again. "We're not like those crazy celebrities who decide to marry in Las Vegas on a whim and regret it the next day. We've lived a long time, your mother and I, and we know our own feelings." He paused to clear his throat. "I'll make your mother happy. I'll love and cherish her until the day I die. I'm not trying to take your father's place, in her heart or in yours. I hope you'll give me a chance to become your friend."

"You could never take my father's place, Mr. Scott," she answered. "And I don't need any more friends."

Stephanie gasped.

"If you know Mom in your heart the way you say, then tell me this. What's her favorite color? What's her favorite movie?" Miranda threw the questions at him like a knight's gauntlet.

James felt his composure slipping. What he wanted most was to give Miranda Andrews a piece of his mind, to tell her how childish she was being, to tell her to think of her mother instead of herself. But he didn't say those things. "The truth is, Miranda, I don't know yet. But it will be my pleasure to learn many of her favorite things the longer she and I are together."

"My father knew the answers." Miranda jutted out her chin. "He could've told you in an instant."

Lord, help me love this stubborn young woman as if she were my own daughter. Help me show her I'm not the enemy.

James drew a deep breath, then met Miranda's hostile gaze with all the gentleness and compassion he could muster. "Your father had five decades with this wonderful woman beside me, and I'd wager he still didn't know everything about her. There are too many secret places in a woman's heart for a man to ever hope to find them all." He turned toward Stephanie, declaring his love once again with his eyes. "I want the chance to discover as many as possible in the years I hope to have with her. I promise I'll do everything humanly possible to make her happy."

"Vince," Miranda said, "please get the children. We're going home."

"Miranda—"

"Mom, you know I'm right. You know you shouldn't marry again this soon. You're just lonely. That's all. Dad was always there to help make the sensible decisions in the family. Well, I'm trying to help you in that way now. Don't do this." Miranda shoved the chair out of her way with the back of her legs, then fled the room in tears.

Vince rose slowly to his feet, setting his napkin on the table. "I'm sorry." He gave a slight shrug. "It's been a rough year since losing her dad so suddenly. She just needs a little more time."

James glanced from Vince to Stephanie and saw doubt flicker across her face. For the first time, he feared what would happen if Miranda didn't change her mind about him. If Stephanie was made to choose between his love or Miranda's, who would win?

CHAPTER TEN

From: "James Scott" <jtscott@fiberpipe.net>
Sent: Wednesday, October 12 3:47 AM
To: "Paula" <carpoolmom@fiberpipe.net>
Subject: October 29 or November 5?

Hi, honey. What did you find out about taking time off at work to come for the wedding? Any problems? We're looking at either the 29th of October or the 5th of November. Could you make those dates? Either? Both? Since neither Kurt nor Jenna said they would come for sure and you did, I thought you should have first choice of the date that's most convenient for you.

I had supper last night at Steph's home with her daughter, Miranda, and her family. I met Miranda's husband, Vince, and their children,

Isabella and Foster, at a high school football
game three weekends ago, but she wasn't able
to be there, so this was our first meeting.

Miranda's reaction to our engagement isn't
good. Worse than Jenna's. She's angry and
thinks we're off our rockers. She didn't use
that old expression, but she may as well have.
Her demeanor said it all. I did my level best
to help her think better of me and our plans
to wed, but I wasn't successful. If anything,
she was more hostile to the idea of our
marriage by the time she left than when she
arrived.

I think she's afraid I'm trying to replace
her father. I'm not. Not in her mind or in the
mind and heart of her mother. I tried to tell
her that, but she was too worked up to listen
to anything I had to say. I'm going to keep
trying to win her over, but it's not going to
be easy. Naturally, all of this is upsetting
to Steph.

As you can see from the time of this email,
I'm up in the middle of the night. Couldn't
sleep. So if you get this before you go to
work and can let me know about the dates ASAP,
it will sure help us make our plans. As soon
as I hear from you, we'll see the pastor and
firm up the wedding plans.

I love you, Paula. Thanks for letting me spout
off. No matter what I say, don't hold anything

against Miranda. We'll work this out between us, just like things will work out with your brother and sister.

Give your girls a hug from their grandpa, and tell them I look forward to seeing them soon.

Dad

The tinkle of bells announced Stephanie's entry into the beauty salon.

From the back room, Terri called, "Is that you, Steph?"

"Yes, it's me."

"Have a seat. I'll be right out. Just throwing a load of towels into the washer."

Stephanie sat on the swivel chair in front of the mirror and glanced at her reflection. Did she look okay? She hadn't slept more than three hours last night, and she hoped her careful application of cosmetics would conceal that fact from others.

Terri entered the main room of the salon just as Stephanie turned the chair away from the mirror. "Hey,

I hear from Frani that congratulations are in order for you and Mr. Scott."

Oh, dear. She'd meant to ask Francine not to tell anyone yet. Not until . . . Until what?

"So when's the big day?"

"A few weeks, we think."

"Wow! It's so romantic. You and your childhood sweetheart, together again." Terri shook out the cape and spread it over Stephanie, fastening it around her neck. "I'm happy for you. Everyone is—or will be as soon as they hear the news."

In her mind, Stephanie pictured her daughter's disapproving glare. *Not everyone.*

She'd hoped Miranda would accept this union once she met James. That hadn't happened. What if it never happened? Would she gain a husband but lose her only child? If there was a risk of losing Miranda's love, should she marry James anyway? What was the right thing to do?

She'd felt better after talking to James yesterday morning, and she'd found courage after praying with Francine. But the supper with Miranda had sent her spirits spiraling into confusion again. She'd been so sure she was doing the right thing when she agreed to marry James. She'd said yes without a moment's hesitation. But now? Now she doubted the wisdom of the choice she'd made.

A doubtful mind, the Bible said, was as unsettled as a wave of the sea that is driven and tossed by the wind. It said that people like that can't make up their minds and they waver back and forth in everything they do.

If ever a verse of Scripture described me, that's it.

"I envy you," Terri said as she led the way to the shampoo bowl, oblivious to Stephanie's tormented thoughts. "I married my childhood sweetheart. Then he treated me like dirt before leaving me and Lyssa for another woman." There wasn't any bitterness in Terri's voice. Just acceptance of fact. "Unlike you, Steph, I won't be having a romantic reunion with the boy who stole my heart when I was a girl. That's for sure." She held the back of the shampoo chair as Stephanie sat down. "I think it's great you two got a second chance. Count yourself blessed."

Stephanie recalled the tenderness of James's gaze, the deep timbre of his laughter, the sweetness of his kisses, the sturdiness of his grasp, and the confidence of his faith. When she was with him, she felt young again, her stomach all aflutter, her heart full of joy. She was blessed. Blessed that he loved her and wanted to marry her.

If not for Miranda . . .

She leaned back in the chair, closed her eyes, and enjoyed the scalp massage Terri gave as she worked the shampoo into a lather.

After a period of silence, Terri asked, "What kind of wedding are you going to have?"

"I haven't really thought about it yet. There hasn't been much time."

"Hope you don't want a small one." Terri ran warm water over her scalp, rinsing away the suds. "All your friends will want to be there. There'll be enough of us to fill the church and then some."

In high school, Stephanie had dreamed about the day she would marry Jimmy Scott. As a teenager, she'd imagined herself walking down the aisle on her daddy's arm, wearing a satin dress covered in pearls and lace, her face hidden behind a beautiful veil.

But Jimmy never proposed. Instead, he went off to the army and college and then asked a different girl to marry him. Stephanie stayed in Hart's Crossing, finished high school, fell in love with Chuck Watson, and married him without a moment's regret.

Perhaps that was supposed to be the end of it. Perhaps Stephanie was in love with the memory of the boy Jimmy had been and not the man James was today.

Was Miranda right after all? Was he a stranger to her? Stephanie thought she loved him, but was she absolutely sure? Perhaps she should have prayed about it a little longer. Wasn't she supposed to have absolute peace when she was doing the right thing? And if so, absence of peace meant she wasn't doing the right thing. Right?

"Steph?"

She opened her eyes and gazed upward. Terri leaned over her, frowning with concern.

"Are you okay?"

"Yes."

"You acted like you couldn't hear me. Are you sure you're all right?"

Stephanie sat upright. "I'm fine. I was lost in thought. That's all."

"Well, okay then." Terri wrapped a towel around Stephanie's head. "If you're sure."

The truth was, she didn't feel sure of anything at the moment.

From:	"Paula Scott" <carpoolmom@fiberpipe.net>
Sent:	Wednesday, October 12 3:15 PM
To:	"Dad" <jtscott@fiberpipe.net>
Subject:	Re: October 29 or November 5?

Hi, Dad. Sorry I couldn't get back to you sooner. I checked on things at work, and it looks like the 29th would be better for both me and the girls. I have enough vacation time saved that we could come early for a nice visit, then leave on Sunday the 30th.

So where will you and Stephanie go on your honeymoon? Make it some place special, Dad. Some place you'll always remember, like Paris.

Better get to work on our reservations.

Love you, Paula

From: "Jenna Scott-Kirkpatrick"
<jscottengland@yahoo.com>

Sent: Wednesday, October 12 6:37 PM

To: "Dad" <jtscott@fiberpipe.net>

Subject: Coming to see you

Dad, I tried to call you several times
yesterday, as promised, but you weren't home.
So I guess I'd better let you know by email
that I've decided to come for a visit after
all. I haven't been back to the States in
two years, and it will be good for you and me
to have some time together. You can show me
around Hart's Crossing. I was just a kid the
last time we went there to see Grandma before
she moved in with us. I don't remember much
about it except there wasn't much to do. So
this will give you a chance to show me what
you love about it.

Looks like I can get a flight for next week.
Don't worry about driving to Twin Falls to
pick me up. I'll get a rental car for the
duration of my stay. All I need from you is a
guest room, and you said you have that.

I still have a few things to work out. As soon
as I've got all the details, I'll send you my
itinerary.

I love you, Dad, and I'm looking forward to
seeing you.

Jenna

James closed his email program and swiveled the
chair so his back was to the computer screen. He was
thankful Paula and her girls could come a few days before the wedding. Jenna's email was another matter. He
didn't need his eldest daughter to spell out the reason
for her hasty trip. She was coming to Hart's Crossing
to make certain he hadn't lost all of his faculties, not
because she hadn't seen him in a couple of years and
most definitely not to celebrate his wedding.

At least Jenna didn't seem angry like Stephanie's
daughter. That was something else he could be thankful for.

He sighed as he rose from the chair and left the
room, walking slowly down the stairs and out to the
porch. A full moon bathed the town in a blanket of
white light.

He wondered why it was hard for some adult children to believe their aging parents could fall in love again. Did they think such feelings were reserved for the young? They weren't. Love was love at any age, and James Scott loved Stephanie Watson.

He recalled the final lines of a favorite poem by John Clare.

> I never saw so sweet a face
> As that I stood before.
> My heart has left its dwelling-place
> And can return no more.

That's what it was like for James. When he looked at Stephanie's sweet face—or, in her absence, when he thought of her—he knew his heart was lost for good. It would never return to him.

Now if only their children could understand that.

CHAPTER ELEVEN

It was a beautiful morning, the air crisp, the sky clear. Fallen leaves crunched beneath Stephanie's sturdy walking shoes as she made her way toward the creek that was lined with cottonwoods and aspens.

For many years, this had been her private getaway, a place she came to think, to read her Bible, and to pray for answers to life's questions. She'd come here when Miranda went through her rebellious teen years. She'd come here when her husband considered a job that would have meant transferring out of state. She'd come here after Chuck's death when she couldn't face another visitor bringing well-meant but empty condolences.

With a sigh, she sat on a large boulder that nature had decorated with soft green moss. Time had also etched a small ledge into the granite, a comfy bench for her feet to rest upon.

As she placed her Bible on her lap, she squinted up through the trees and whispered, "Lord, show me what to do. I know what I want, but I don't seem to know what's right. What is it you want for me?"

The place to begin, she supposed, was with love. God's will always included love. She turned to 1 Corinthians.

Stephanie and Chuck, like countless other couples before and since, had used these words from the thirteenth chapter in their wedding ceremony. She'd read them many times, sometimes with joy, more often with conviction at how far from the mark she continued to fall. How seldom—if ever—did she love the way God called her to love.

Love was patient and kind, the Word told her. Love wasn't jealous or boastful or proud or rude, and it didn't demand its own way. It wasn't irritable, and it kept no record of when it was wronged. Love was never glad about injustice but rejoiced whenever the truth won out. Love never gave up and never lost faith. Love was always hopeful, enduring through every circumstance.

"I loved Chuck with all my heart. I tried to be a good wife always. And I love my daughter unconditionally. She must know that. Doesn't she?" Stephanie drew a slow, deep breath. "Lord Jesus, I love James, too. I want to be with him. But if marrying him costs me Miranda's love . . ."

She riffled the well-worn pages with her left thumb and stopped when her eyes fell on an orange highlighted portion.

So the person who marries does well, it read, *and the person who doesn't marry does even better. A wife is married to her husband as long as he lives. If her husband dies, she is free to marry whomever she wishes, but this must be a marriage acceptable to the Lord.*

Stephanie's heart fluttered. A person who marries does well. A widow is free to marry whomever she wishes, as long as God approves.

123

"Is this marriage to James acceptable to you, Lord? He belongs to you, so we wouldn't be unequally yoked. Is this your will for me?"

She read on: *But in my opinion it will be better for her if she doesn't marry again, and I think I am giving you counsel from God's Spirit when I say this.*

She felt great irritation with the apostle Paul for adding that line. She wanted a clear, absolute, positive instruction, and what the apostle wrote, he said, was his opinion. She didn't want his opinion. She wanted an unmistakable answer. She wanted guidance, a clear, distinct path, like the trail she had followed to reach this creek.

"Jesus, I need to hear your voice."

Love never gives up, came the whisper in her heart.

Yes. That was true. But was it love for James that should never give up or was it love for her daughter that was to be her first priority?

Or was it possible that the two could be one and the same?

James told himself not to worry when he tried for the fifth time that morning to call Stephanie and got no answer. He told himself that he wasn't her keeper when he stopped by her house just after 1:00 and found her still not at home. As he drove into town for a late lunch, he watched for her car at Francine Hunter's home, in the Smith's Market parking lot, and along the curb outside Terri's Tangles; he didn't see it anywhere.

Where could she be?

The Over the Rainbow Diner was empty of the lunch crowd by the time James arrived. Nancy Raney greeted him with her usual warm smile and escorted him to a booth.

"Anything besides water to drink?" she asked.

"A Diet Coke, please, Nancy."

"Sure thing. Back in a flash."

James took a menu from the rack and glanced at it. Nothing looked appetizing.

Where is she?

James and Stephanie had spoken by telephone twice yesterday, once before she left to have her hair done and again in the evening when he phoned to tell her that Jenna would be arriving for a visit the following week. Both times he'd felt Stephanie pulling away. He knew why—a safety measure, of sorts, in case things didn't work out between them.

Yes, he knew why, but he didn't know what he could do about it. He didn't know how to make her believe all would be well.

And if he couldn't make her believe it, maybe everything *wouldn't* be well. Maybe her worries would become a self-fulfilling prophecy.

Nancy arrived at his table, Coke glass in one hand, water glass in the other. "Have you decided?" she asked as she set the beverages before him.

"I'll have a toasted BLT."

"Wheat or white bread?"

"Wheat, please."

"Soup or salad?"

When a man ate from habit rather than hunger, he didn't want to make choices. "Surprise me."

She laughed. "You got it."

After Nancy headed for the kitchen, James turned his gaze out the window, looking across Main Street at the Apollo. He had lots of memories of that old theater, and many of them included Stephanie. Saturday matinees with black-and-white westerns flickering on the screen. V-J Day with its wild celebrations. Friday night dates when they were in high school and they'd talked about what they wanted to be and where they wanted to live.

He'd loved Stephanie Carlson, but he hadn't been ready for marriage when he was eighteen. Now, at the ripe old age of seventy, he was ready for it. More than ready.

He couldn't explain how or why this love for her had blossomed so quickly since his return. He only knew it had. He knew that it was real, solid, and lasting. It was an old love, yet it was like first love, too. He wanted to spend the rest of his days with Stephanie. He wanted to read love poetry to her by the fire on cold winter nights. He wanted to stroll with her through town on soft summer evenings. He wanted to be her husband, her lover, her best friend. God willing, they would have many good and healthy years together.

But first he had to keep her from bolting like a scared colt.

"You look like you could use a friend, Jimmy Scott."

He turned from the window as Till Hart slid onto the seat across from him. With a shake of his head, he said, "Is my mood that obvious?"

"Mmm. I'd say so."

"I don't suppose you've talked to Steph today. I haven't been able to reach her."

"Sorry. I haven't seen or talked to her all week. Not since you whisked her away to a fancy lunch at the resort and proposed marriage—or so I hear tell from Frani." Till clucked her tongue. "You certainly didn't let any grass grow under your feet, James. I'll say that for you."

He tried to smile but failed.

"You don't look like a happy groom-to-be. Why is that?"

"Our kids," he answered solemnly. "Except for my youngest, they don't approve of our wedding plans." He glanced down at his hands clenched into fists atop the table. "I don't mind getting old, Till. I can deal with the aches and pains that come with age. I figure

I've earned them, living this long. But I resent being treated like a child by my own offspring."

"I believe I would, too."

"But that's not the worst part." He looked up again. "I'm afraid Steph's having second thoughts. I'm afraid Miranda and Jenna's attitudes are going to drive a wedge between us, and I don't know how to stop it from happening."

"Oh, dear. We mustn't let that happen. Not if you and Steph love each other."

"We do, Till. I guarantee it."

That evening, Till Hart called an emergency meeting of the Thimbleberry Quilting Club. If there was one thing the members of this group knew how to do even better than creating beautiful quilts, it was how to pray.

Through the years, they—and many former members of the club—had prayed for one another, for family and friends, and for complete strangers. They'd prayed when couples married, when babies were born, and when folks died. They'd prayed for elections, wars, and natural disasters in America and far corners of the world. They'd prayed for circumstances that seemed overwhelming, and they'd prayed for secret wishes of the heart. From the eldest member to the youngest, they were women who believed in the power of prayer and in a God who delighted in giving good gifts to his children.

On that evening in mid-October, five of the six Thimbleberry members—only Stephanie was absent and that was by design—gathered in the living room of Till's home to pray for their dear friend and for the man who loved her.

CHAPTER TWELVE

Stephanie had prayed that she would hear God's voice and know what she was to do, and early the next morning, in that halfway state between waking and sleeping, she received an answer.

And the Lord God said, "It is not good for the man to be alone. I will make a companion who will help him."

As the verse from Genesis floated through her mind, Stephanie opened her eyes, half expecting to see someone else in the room because the voice seemed so clear.

I made you, beloved, for a purpose.

Her pulse quickened.

I made you to be his companion.

Despite the rapid beating of her heart, Stephanie felt at peace. The special peace that came only from knowing and doing God's will. Rare moments like this, when God spoke directly to her spirit, left her breathless with wonder. She heard and she understood. There was no room left for doubt.

She slid upright against the headboard and reached for the telephone on her nightstand. After punching in the number, she waited impatiently for an answer on the other end of the line.

Her heart skipped when she heard his sleepy, "Hello?"

"James, it's me."

"Steph?" He sounded more alert. "Thank God. Are you all right? Where were you yesterday? I kept calling, but you never answered the phone."

"I'm fine. Really. I needed to go off by myself for the day. I had some praying and soul searching to do."

Silence, then, "And?"

She smiled, hoping he could hear it in her voice. "And the children will simply have to accept that we're getting married." She brought her lips closer to the mouthpiece. "I love you, James. I want to be your wife more than anything."

"Don't go anywhere. Do you hear me? I'm getting dressed and coming right over. Don't go anywhere."

Stephanie looked at the clock. "It's only 6:30."

"I don't care. I'm up and you're up. What the clock reads doesn't matter to us."

She laughed softly. "All right. I'll put the coffee on. Come to the back door. It'll be unlocked."

The moment she hung up the phone, Stephanie tossed aside the bedcovers and hurried to the bathroom to wash her face, brush her teeth, and run a brush through her hair. She changed into a pair of slacks and a blouse, then went to the kitchen to make the coffee. It was just starting to brew when a soft rap sounded. An instant later, the back door opened.

If there had been any shred of doubt remaining about her decision to marry James, it would have disappeared at the sight of him. Her heart skipped, and she felt as giddy as she had at the age of sixteen when he arrived, clad in tux and cummerbund, to escort her to the junior-senior prom.

Strange, the pathways of life. She had loved James twice—first as a girl, then as an old woman. Yes, they were strange . . . wonderful . . . unexplainable, the pathways that had brought her back to him. No wonder her daughter couldn't understand what had happened in the past few weeks. Stephanie barely understood it herself.

"You're beautiful in the morning," James said.

Beautiful? Perhaps in her youth, but no more. Now her face was wrinkled, her hair was Ivory soap white, and her body was soft in too many of the wrong places. But as James drew near, she realized he meant what he said. She *was* beautiful in his eyes.

He gathered her in his arms. Arms still strong despite his age. Strong enough to hold her close. "You had me worried for a while. I was afraid I'd lose you."

"I know. I'm sorry."

One day she would share with him the words God had whispered to her. Perhaps on their anniversary as they reminisced about their whirlwind second courtship.

James kissed her softly on the mouth, and when their lips parted, Stephanie sighed with pleasure. Romantic love was not the property of the young, no matter what people believed.

"Tell me something," he said.

"Of course."

"What's your favorite color?"

She smiled as she touched his jaw, running her fingers over his close-trimmed beard. "It's a tie. Aquamarine and lemon yellow."

"And your favorite movie?"

"Sound of Music."

It pleased her that he'd remembered Miranda's questions. It pleased her that it mattered to him because it mattered to her daughter. It made her believe things would be well between Miranda and James. If not this week or next week, then perhaps next month or the one after that.

James brushed his lips against her forehead. "We'd better call John Gunn this morning and arrange for the church."

"Yes. I think we'd better. I'm ready to become Mrs. James Scott." She looked up at him. "The sooner, the better."

CHAPTER THIRTEEN

Twelve days later, the Thimbleberry Quilting Club hosted a bridal shower for Stephanie in the fellowship hall of Hart's Crossing Community Church. It was a joyous affair.

Francine and Angie Hunter led the guests in a few silly games that had everyone in stitches. Then they all clapped and teased as Stephanie opened her gifts, including a beautiful aquamarine negligee and robe. Afterward, the guests drank punch and ate cake while Till Hart regaled them with long-ago stories about Stephanie. One thing could be said about Till—there was nothing wrong with her memory!

"Mom!" Miranda exclaimed, looking at her with wide eyes after hearing about the night a bunch of kids from the junior class drove fifty miles to steal their arch rival's school mascot. "Did you really do that?"

"Well, it wasn't only me." Stephanie cast a mock glare in Till's direction. "There were a dozen of us involved."

"I can't believe you'd do such a thing." Miranda shook her head. "It's just not like you."

Interesting, how parents were viewed by their children. Stephanie had no trouble seeing her involvement in that high school episode as being "just like her." She hadn't been what anyone would call wild, but she'd pulled her share of teenage pranks that got her in hot water.

Paula, seated on Stephanie's left side, leaned close and whispered, "No wonder Daddy fell in love with you. You rascal, you."

Although Paula had been Stephanie and James's greatest ally from the moment she and her daughters stepped onto the tarmac at the Twin Falls airport, the past week had seen a softening of attitudes with the other three children as well, giving Stephanie hope that one day the two families would become truly united.

Miranda had begun to warm up to James, despite herself. The more time they spent together, the less angry Miranda was and the less she seemed to fear that he wanted to replace her father. It was a good beginning.

Jenna had arrived in Hart's Crossing, expecting to find a treasure-hunting black widow who had trapped her unsuspecting father in a web. It hadn't taken long for Jenna to learn that Stephanie was anything but. While still not thrilled that her father had chosen to marry so quickly, neither had she raised more opposition.

As for the pragmatic Kurt, he'd accepted the inevitable with a "If you're sure, Dad," and a "Welcome to the family, Stephanie."

Most importantly, over the past few days, each of their children had let their parents know, in ways both large and small, that they were loved. And love, Stephanie knew, would see all of them through. Love never failed.

How blessed she was, she thought as she looked around the fellowship hall, to be surrounded by family and friends, some who had prayed for her countless times through the years, loved ones who'd lifted her when she had no strength to stand on her own. God had been good to her. He'd given her fifty years with her beloved Chuck. He'd entrusted her with their wonderful daughter. And now he'd brought James back into her life.

Autumn had always been Stephanie's favorite season of the year—and now she thought it might become the favorite season of her life as well.

Who, besides God, knew what the future held in store?

Storms? Probably.

Love? Most assuredly.

Stephanie couldn't wait for the adventure to begin.

A sneak peek at Book 3 of the Hart's Crossing series

Diamond Place

Nobody loved baseball more than ten-year-old Lyssa Sampson. Nobody. As far as she was concerned, there was only one season of the year—baseball season. Lyssa's bedroom walls were covered with posters of her favorite players. Instead of dolls, she collected baseball caps from the major league teams. She memorized stats and read every issue of *Baseball Digest* from cover to cover.

If there was one thing her young heart desired more than anything else, it was to be the Hart's Crossing Cavaliers' starting pitcher this year. Just one thing stood in her way—Coach Jenkins. Somehow she had to convince him that she was good enough to take their Little League team to the championships.

Maybe if her mom would be nicer to him . . .

A native Idahoan, **Robin Lee Hatcher** loves to share her passion for God through the books she writes. She is the best-selling author of more than forty-five contemporary and historical novels, including *Beyond the Shadows*, *Legacy Lane*, and *Catching Katie*. Her many awards include the Christy Award for Excellence in Christian Fiction and the RITA Award for Best Inspirational Romance. Robin is a frequent speaker at writers' conferences and Christian women's retreats. When not writing or traveling, she revels in her roles of wife, mom, and grandma. She and her husband live in Boise with their three dogs and one aristocratic cat.

Watch for more news from

HART'S CROSSING
the small town with the big heart